The Emperor's New Clothes

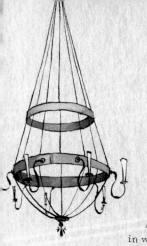

Graphic Spin is published by Stone Arch Books,
A Capstone Imprint
151 Good Counsel Drive, P.O. Box 669
Mankato, Minnesota 56002
www.capstonepub.com

Library of Congress Cataloging-in-Publication Data

Peters, Stephanie True, 1965-
  The Emperor's new clothes : the graphic novel / by Hans Christian Andersen ;
retold by Stephanie Peters ; illustrated by Jeffrey Stewart Timmins.
    p. cm. -- (Graphic spin)
  ISBN 978-1-4342-1595-6 (lib. bdg.) -- ISBN 978-1-4342-1744-8 (pbk.)
  1. Graphic novels. [1. Graphic novels. 2. Fairy tales.] I. Timmins, Jeffrey Stewart,
ill. II. Andersen, H. C. (Hans Christian), 1805-1875. Kejserens nye klæder. III.
Title.
  PZ7.7.P44Em 2010
  741.5'973--dc22

                        2009010528

  Summary: In a faraway kingdom, there lives an emperor who prizes fancy clothes
above all else. He buys suit after suit made of the most expensive materials instead
of tending to his threadbare kingdom. Then, one day, two traveling merchants offer
to make the emperor a special suit that has magical powers. The merchants, however,
are not who they claim to be, and the suit has one major flaw — no one can see it!

Graphic Designer: Carla Zetina-Yglesias

3 9547 00345 4605

Printed in the United States of America in Stevens Point, Wisconsin.
032010
005744R

GRAPHIC
NOVEL

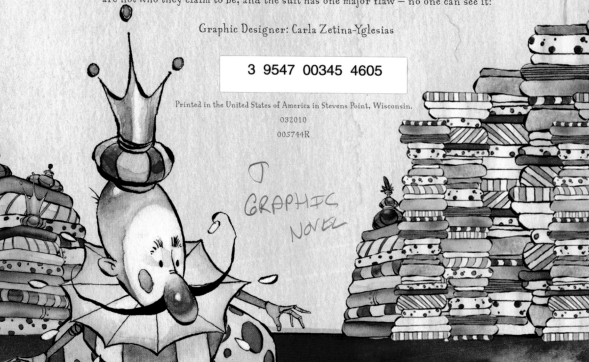

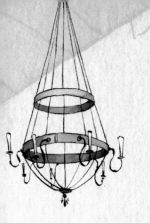
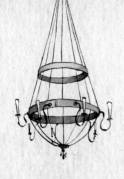
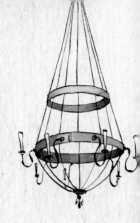

HANS CHRISTIAN ANDERSON'S

The Emperor's New Clothes

THE GRAPHIC NOVEL

retold by
Stephanie True Peters

illustrated by
Jeffrey Stewart Timmins

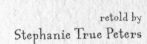

STONE ARCH BOOKS
MINNEAPOLIS   SAN DIEGO

Cast of Characters

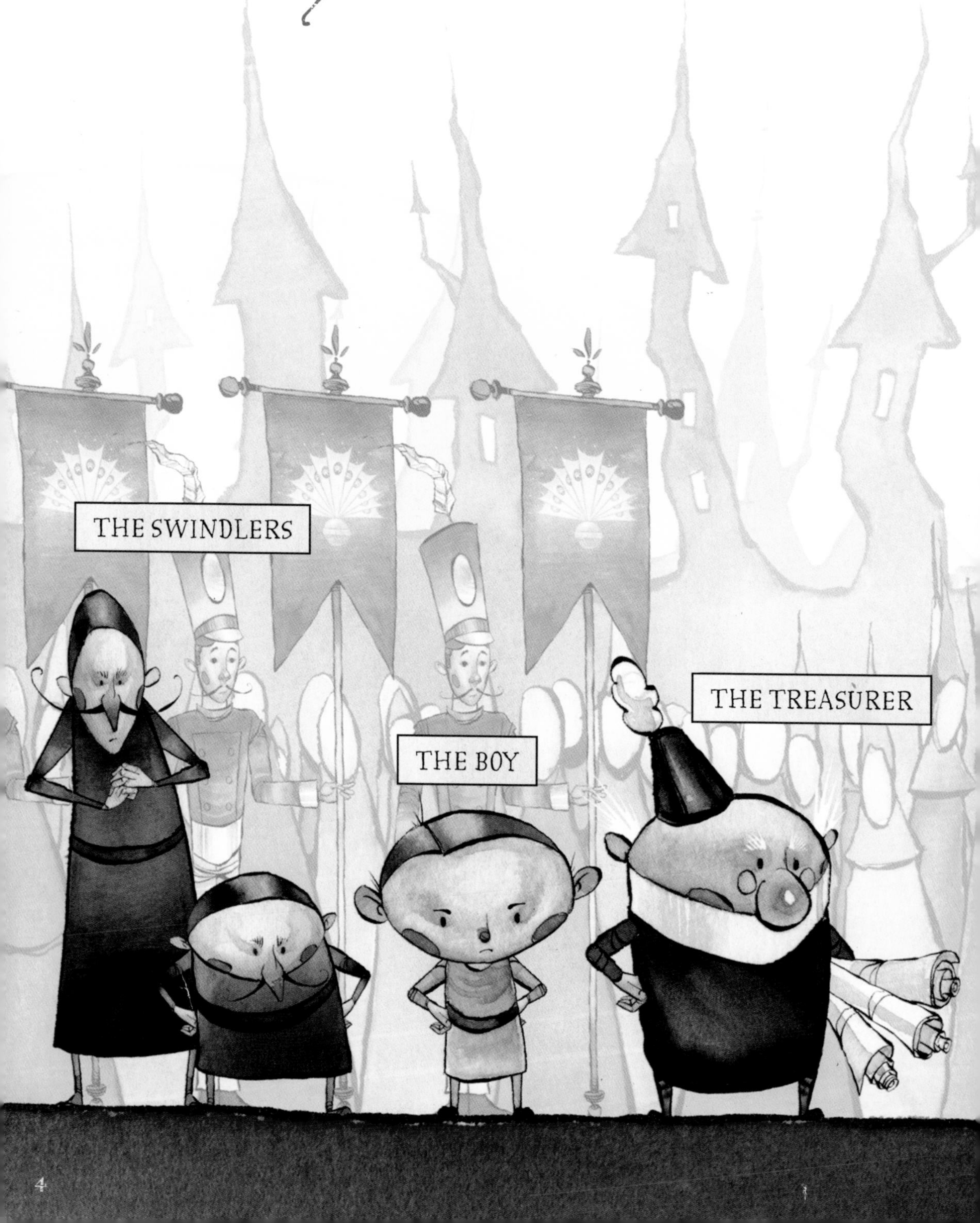
THE SWINDLERS
THE BOY
THE TREASURER

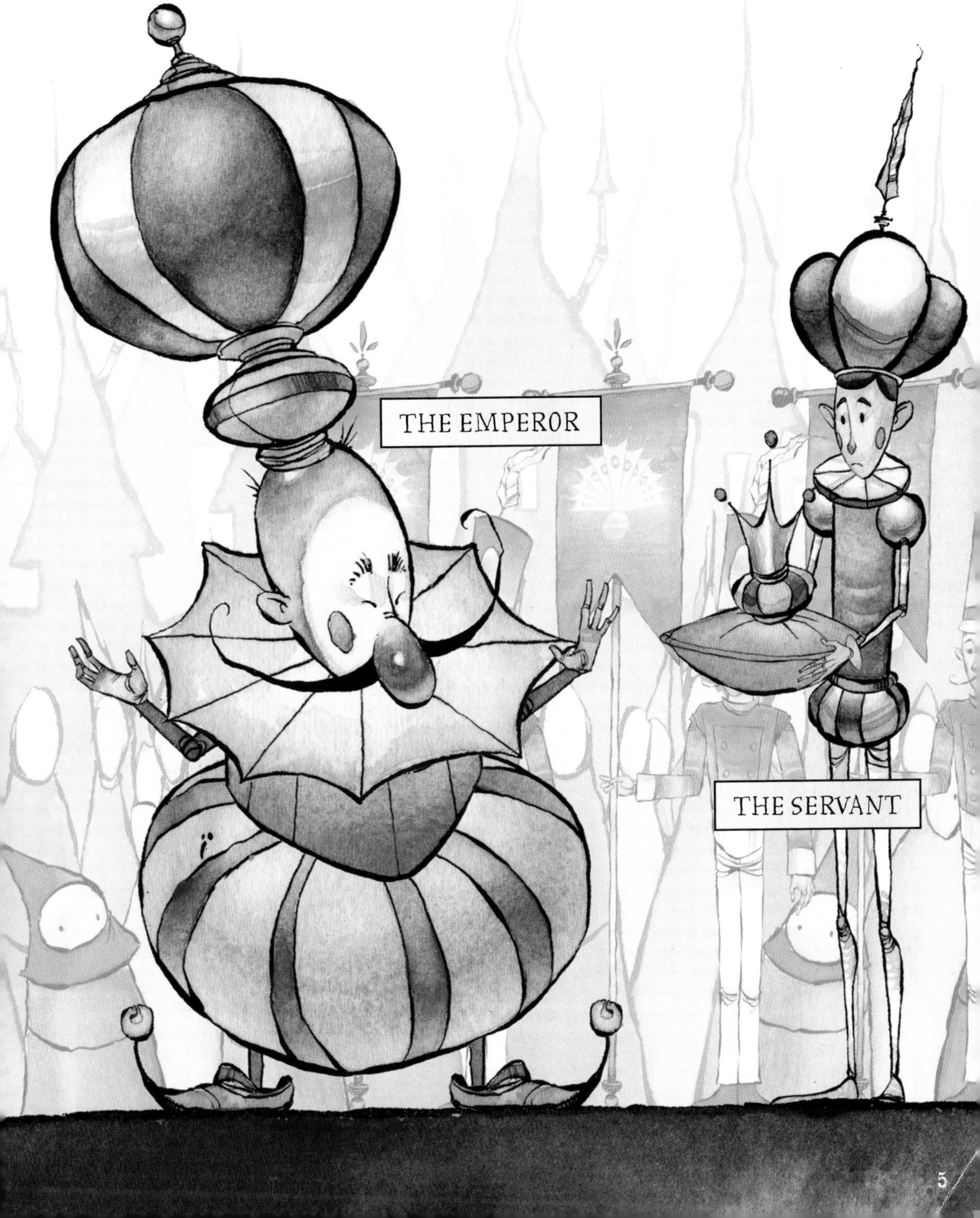
THE EMPEROR
THE SERVANT

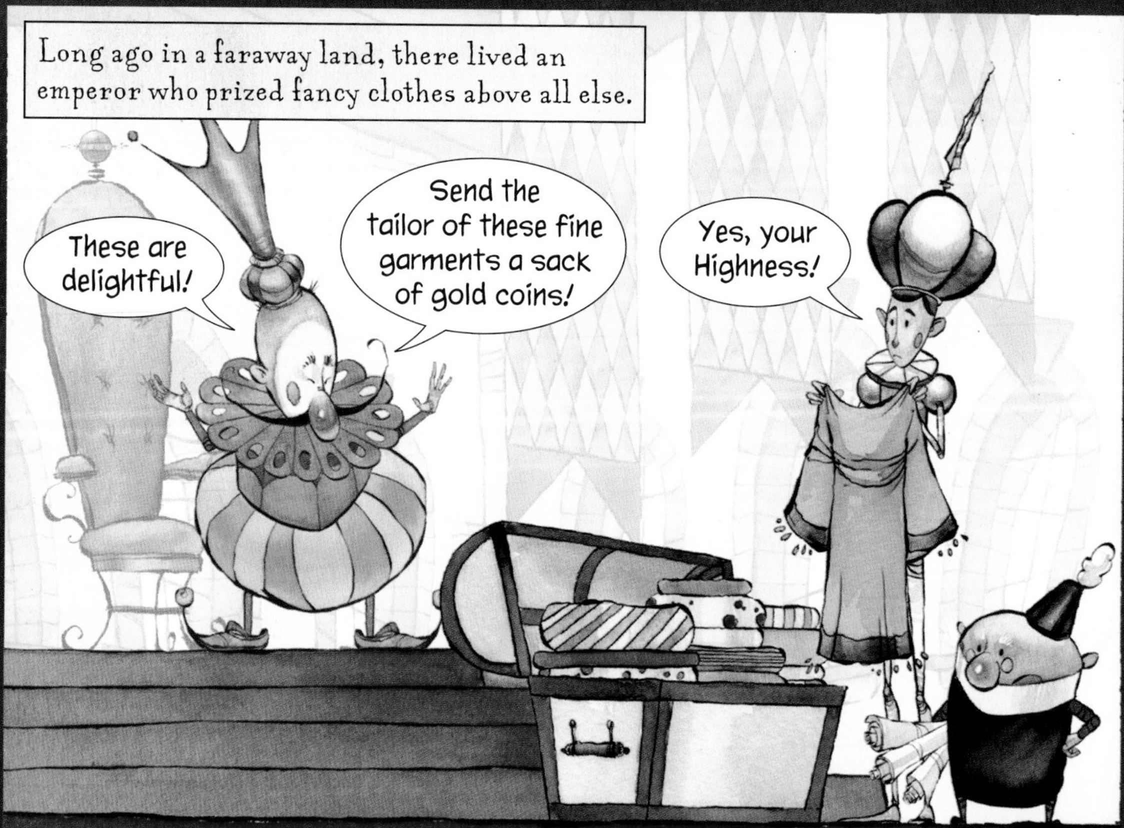

Long ago in a faraway land, there lived an emperor who prized fancy clothes above all else.
These are delightful!
Send the tailor of these fine garments a sack of gold coins!
Yes, your Highness!

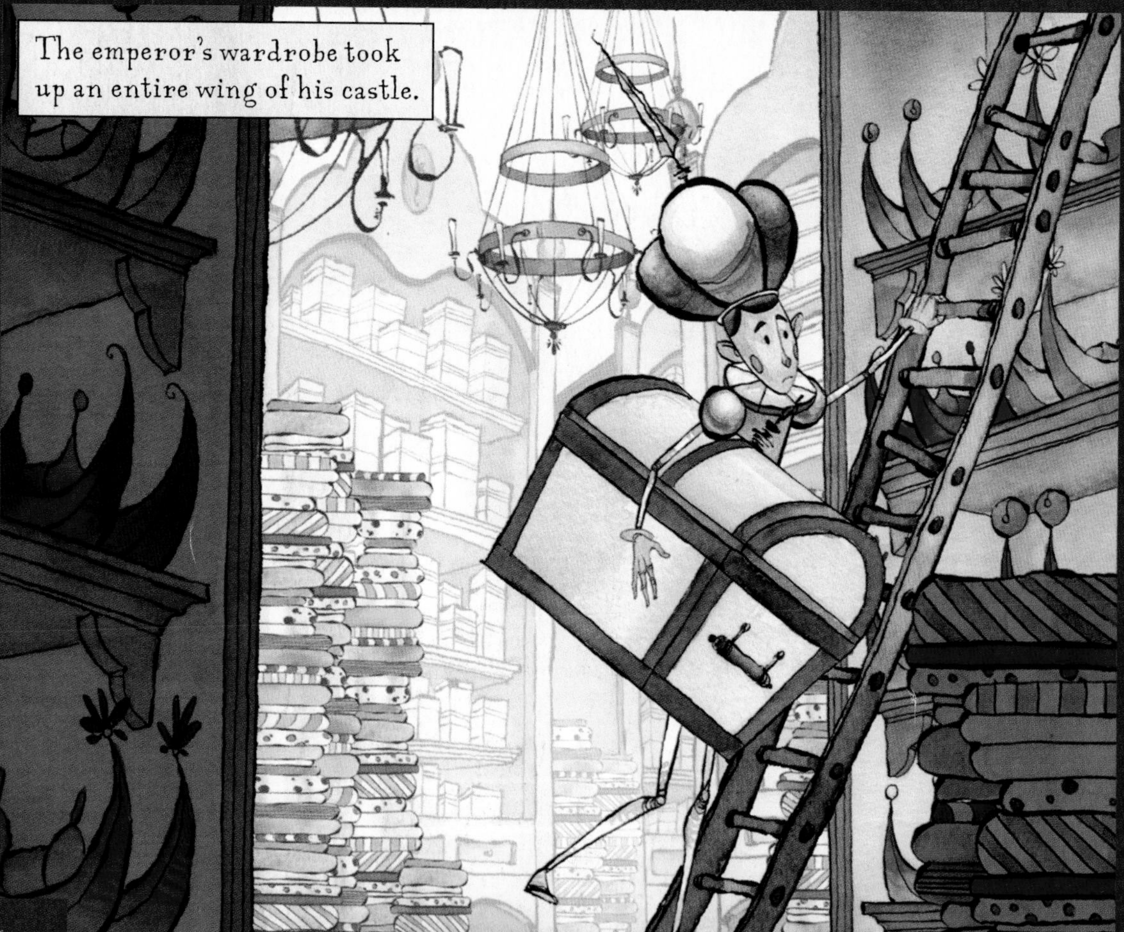

The emperor's wardrobe took up an entire wing of his castle.

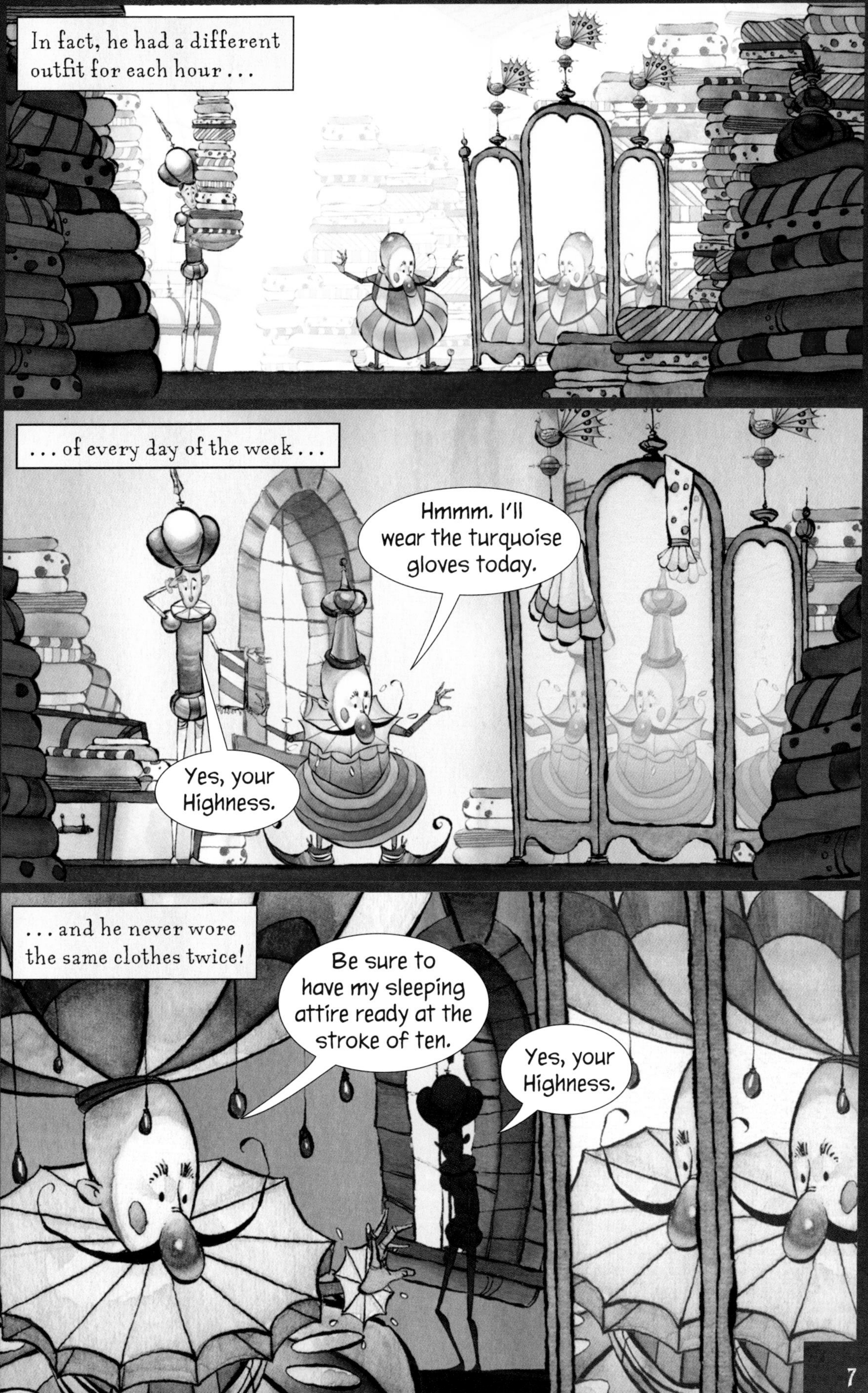

In fact, he had a different outfit for each hour . . .
. . . of every day of the week . . .
Hmmm. I'll wear the turquoise gloves today.
Yes, your Highness.
. . . and he never wore the same clothes twice!
Be sure to have my sleeping attire ready at the stroke of ten.
Yes, your Highness.

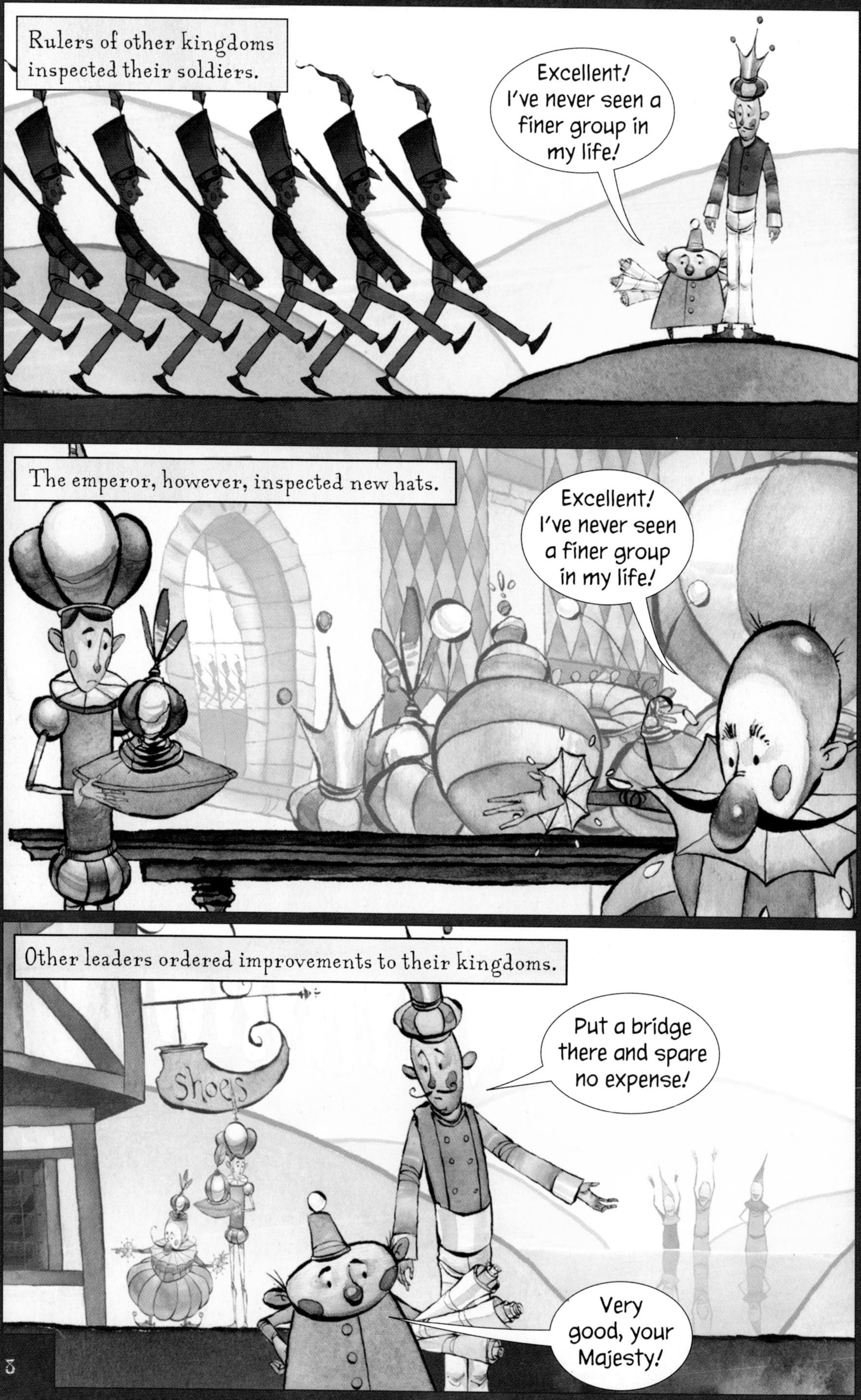
Rulers of other kingdoms inspected their soldiers.
Excellent! I've never seen a finer group in my life!
The emperor, however, inspected new hats.
Excellent! I've never seen a finer group in my life!
Other leaders ordered improvements to their kingdoms.
Shoes
Put a bridge there and spare no expense!
Very good, your Majesty!

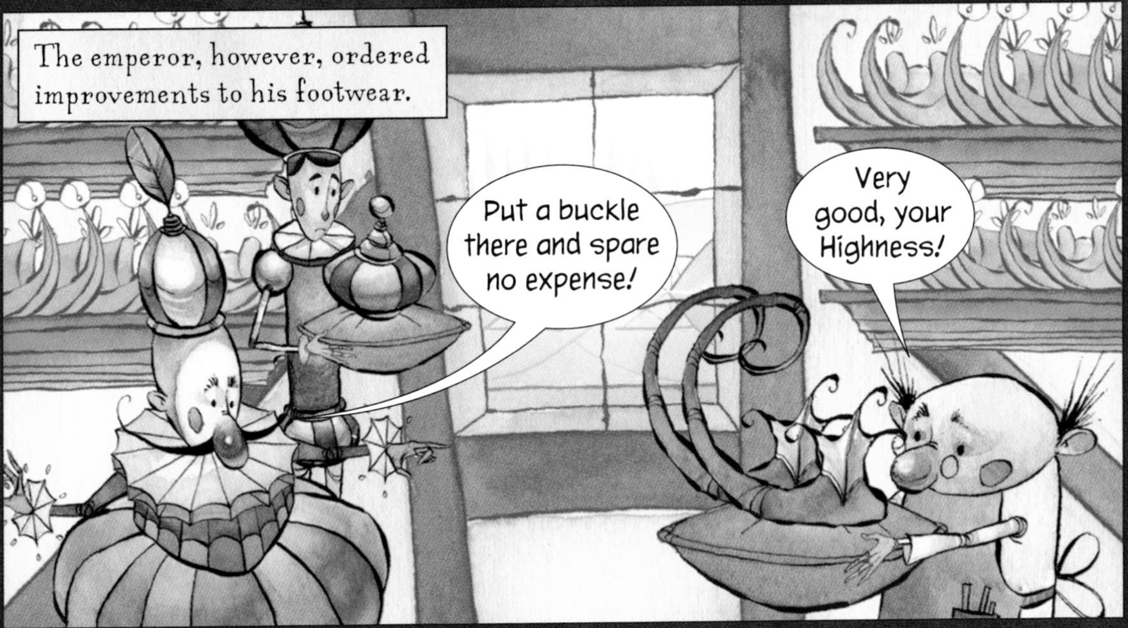
The emperor, however, ordered improvements to his footwear.
Put a buckle there and spare no expense!
Very good, your Highness!

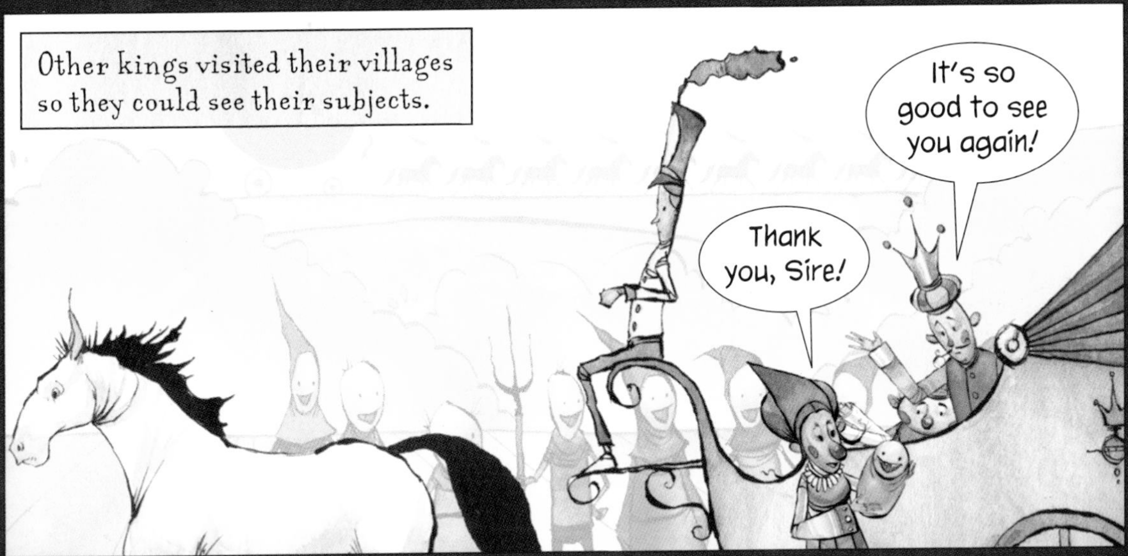
Other kings visited their villages so they could see their subjects.
It's so good to see you again!
Thank you, Sire!

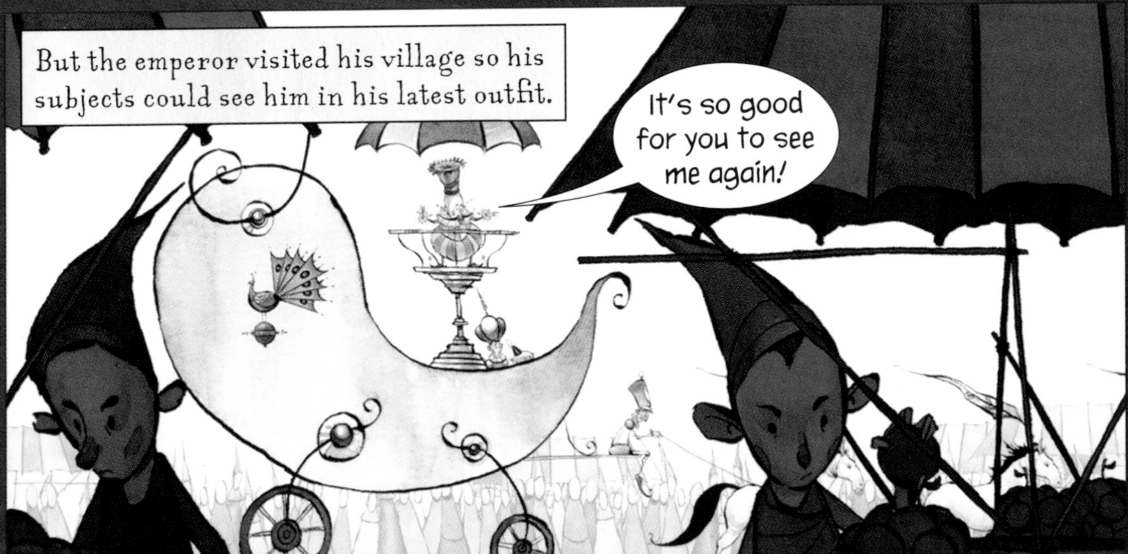
But the emperor visited his village so his subjects could see him in his latest outfit.
It's so good for you to see me again!

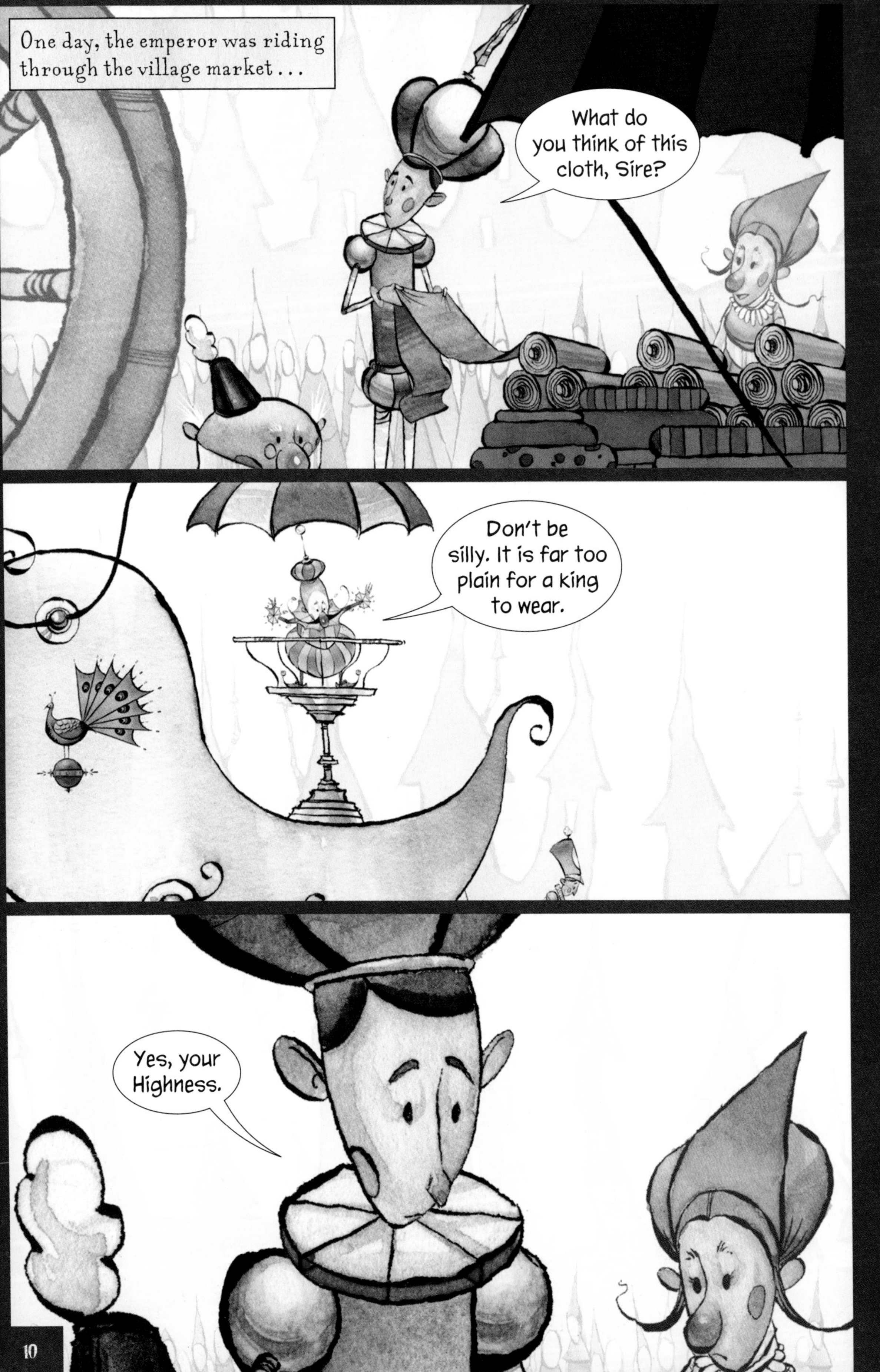
One day, the emperor was riding through the village market . . .
What do you think of this cloth, Sire?
Don't be silly. It is far too plain for a king to wear.
Yes, your Highness.

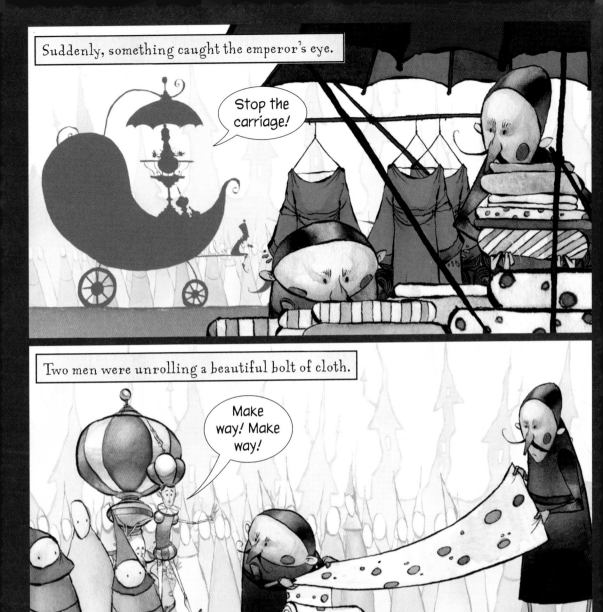

Suddenly, something caught the emperor's eye.

Stop the carriage!

Two men were unrolling a beautiful bolt of cloth.

Make way! Make way!

The emperor was delighted with the cloth that he saw.

Such fine work! You are truly expert weavers!

Thank you, your Highness.

Yes, thank you.

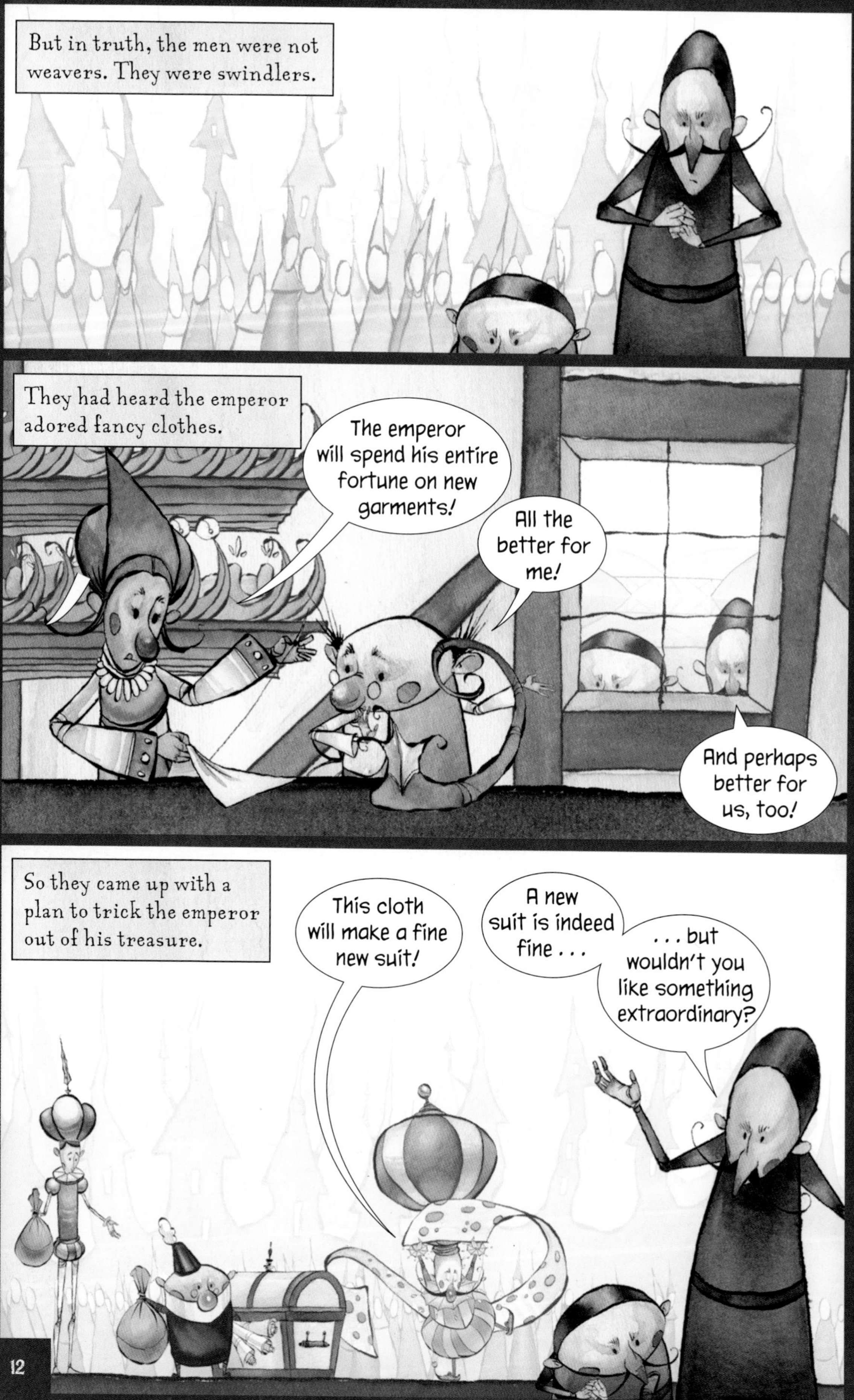
But in truth, the men were not weavers. They were swindlers.
They had heard the emperor adored fancy clothes.
The emperor will spend his entire fortune on new garments!
All the better for me!
And perhaps better for us, too!
So they came up with a plan to trick the emperor out of his treasure.
This cloth will make a fine new suit!
A new suit is indeed fine . . .
. . . but wouldn't you like something extraordinary?

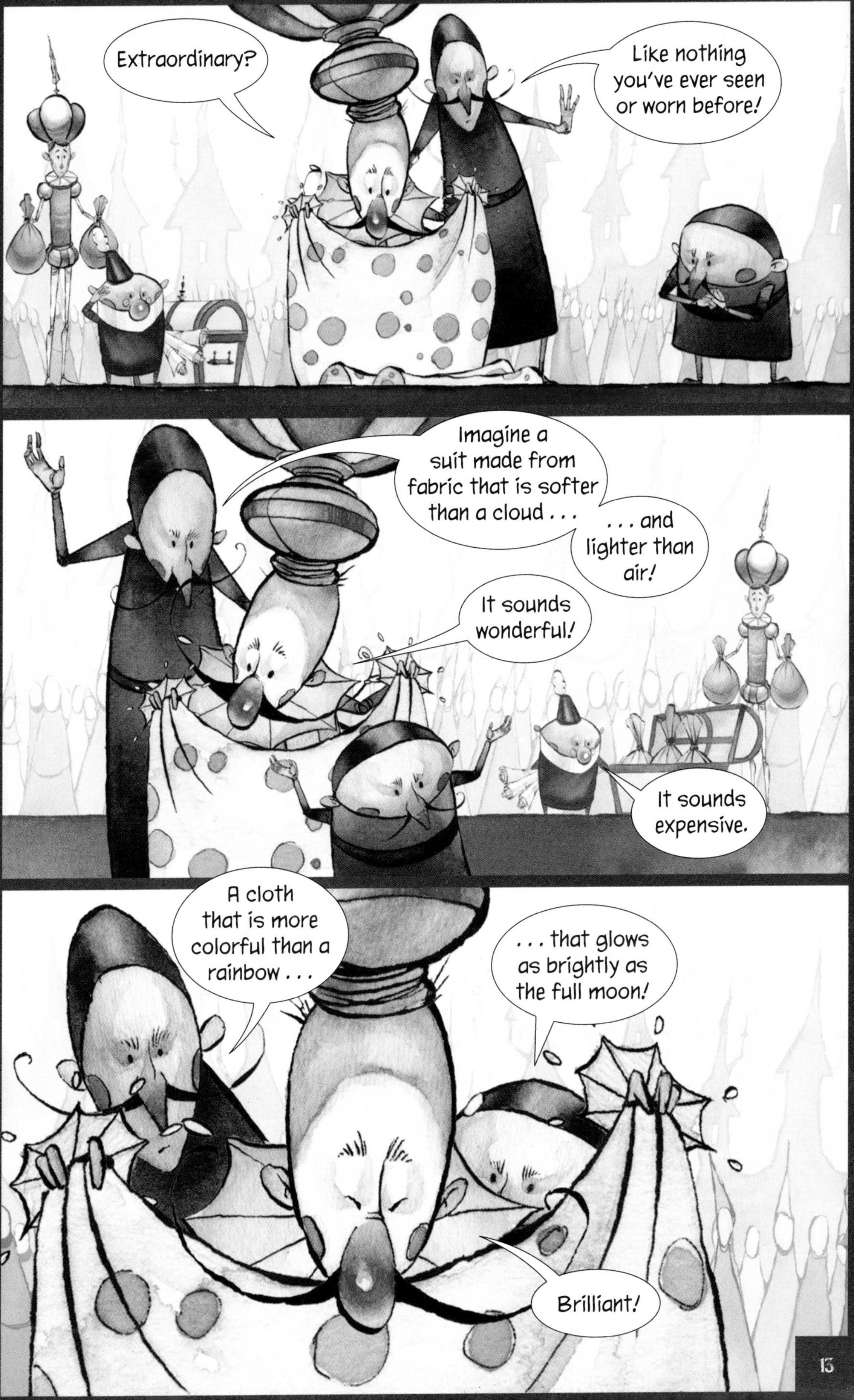
Extraordinary?
Like nothing you've ever seen or worn before!
Imagine a suit made from fabric that is softer than a cloud . . .
. . . and lighter than air!
It sounds wonderful!
It sounds expensive.
A cloth that is more colorful than a rainbow . . .
. . . that glows as brightly as the full moon!
Brilliant!

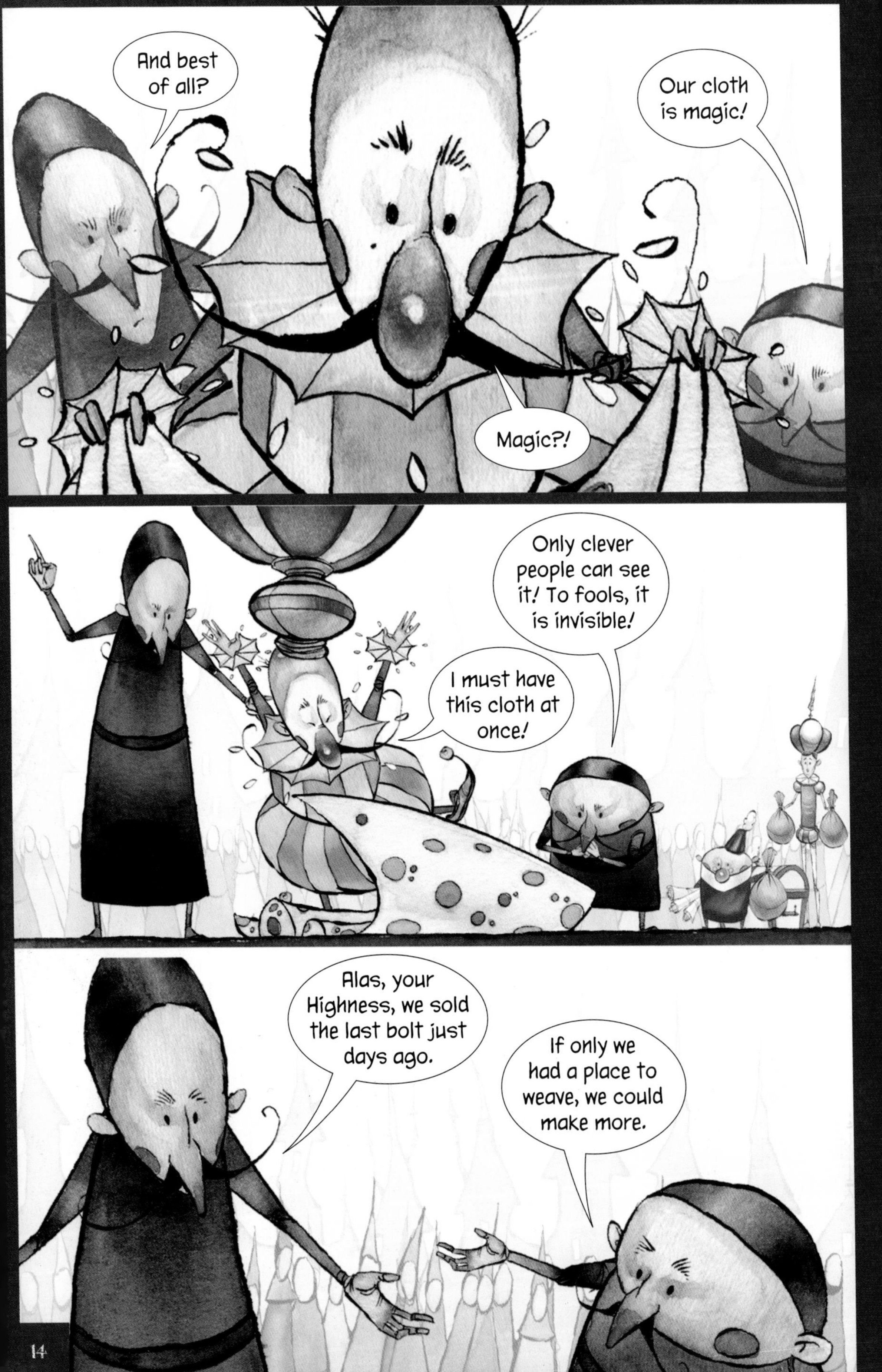
And best of all?
Our cloth is magic!
Magic?!
Only clever people can see it! To fools, it is invisible!
I must have this cloth at once!
Alas, your Highness, we sold the last bolt just days ago.
If only we had a place to weave, we could make more.

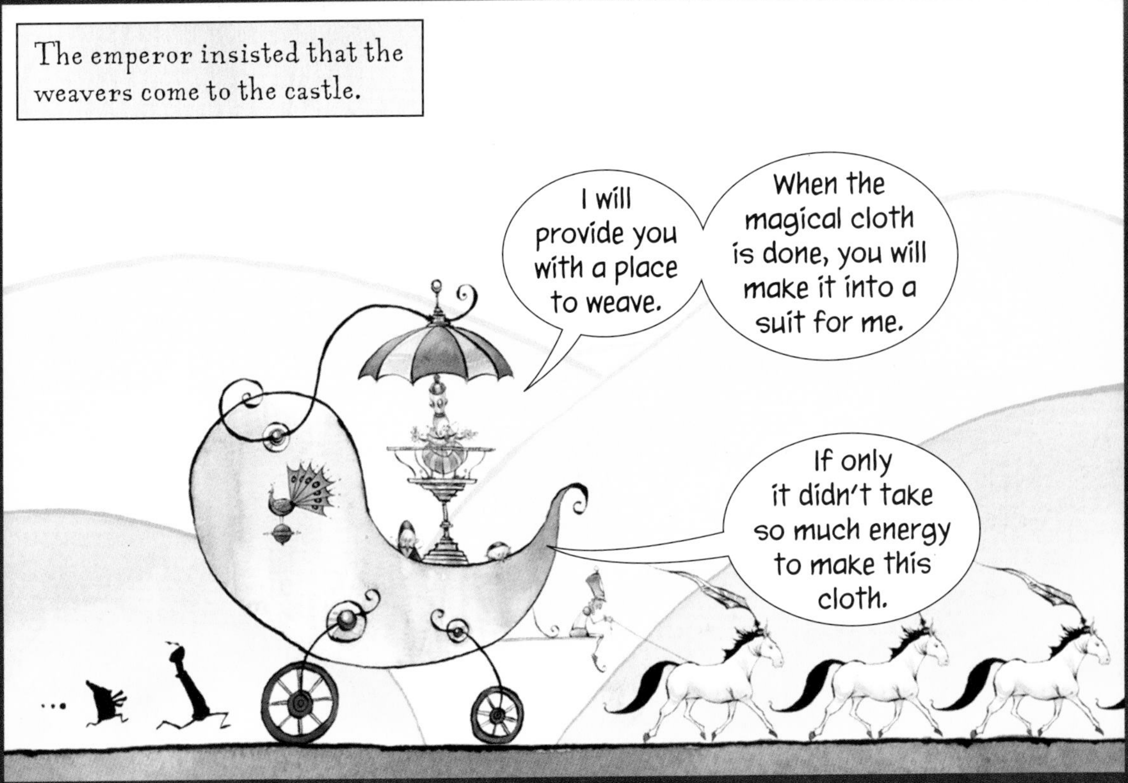
The emperor insisted that the weavers come to the castle.
I will provide you with a place to weave.
When the magical cloth is done, you will make it into a suit for me.
If only it didn't take so much energy to make this cloth.

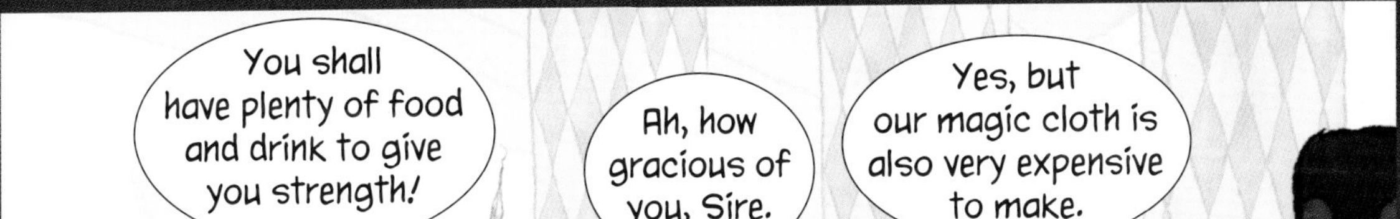
You shall have plenty of food and drink to give you strength!
Ah, how gracious of you, Sire.
Yes, but our magic cloth is also very expensive to make.

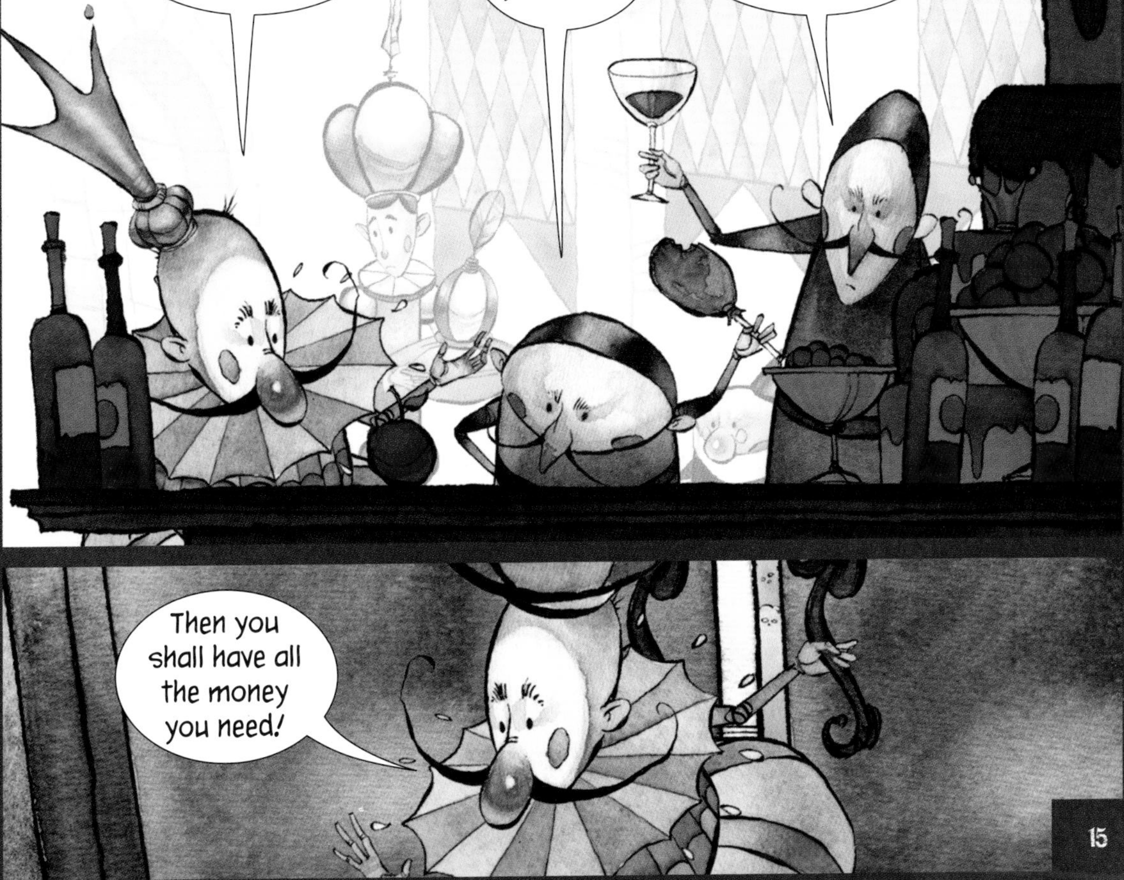
Then you shall have all the money you need!

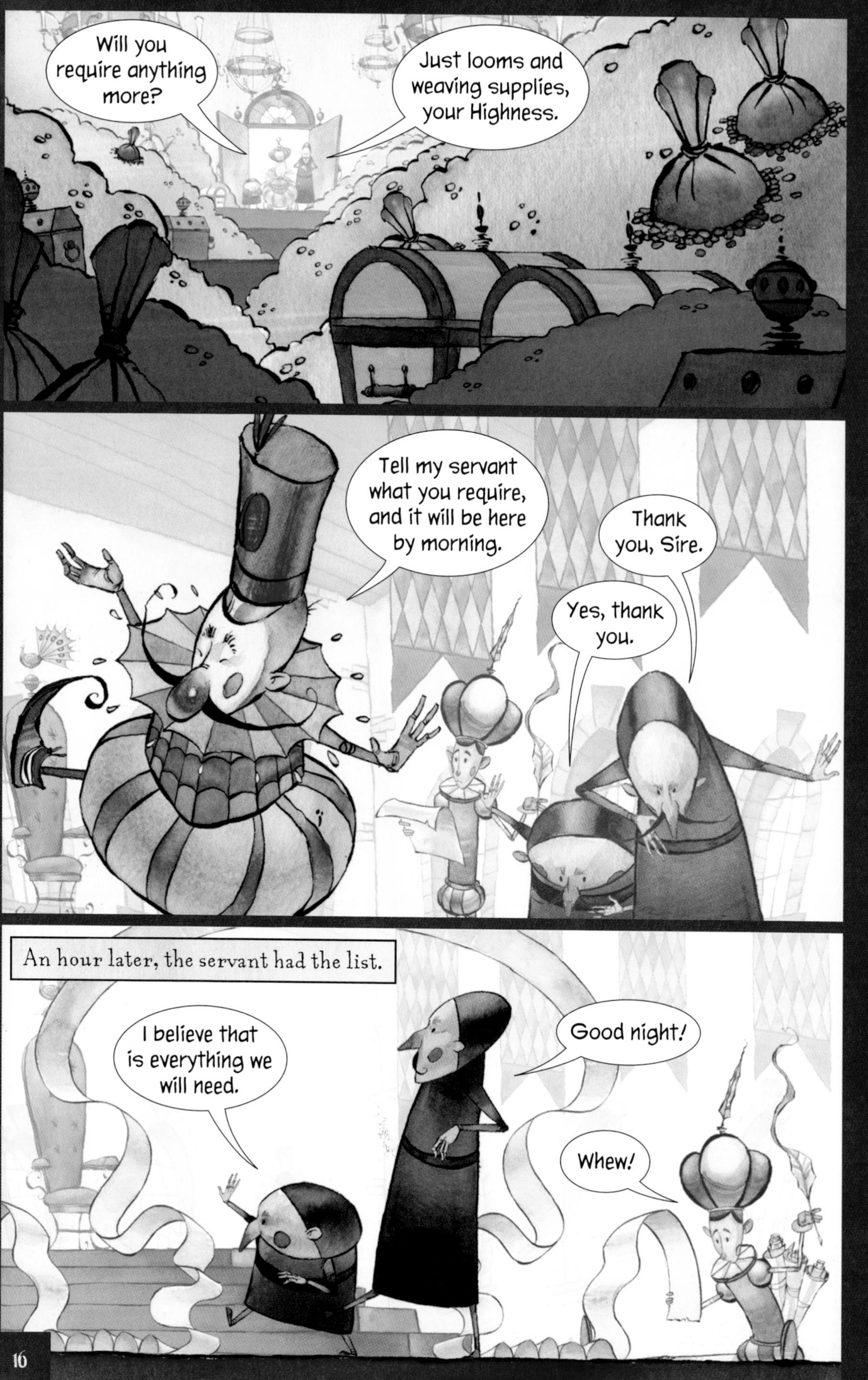
Will you require anything more?
Just looms and weaving supplies, your Highness.
Tell my servant what you require, and it will be here by morning.
Thank you, Sire.
Yes, thank you.
An hour later, the servant had the list.
I believe that is everything we will need.
Good night!
Whew!

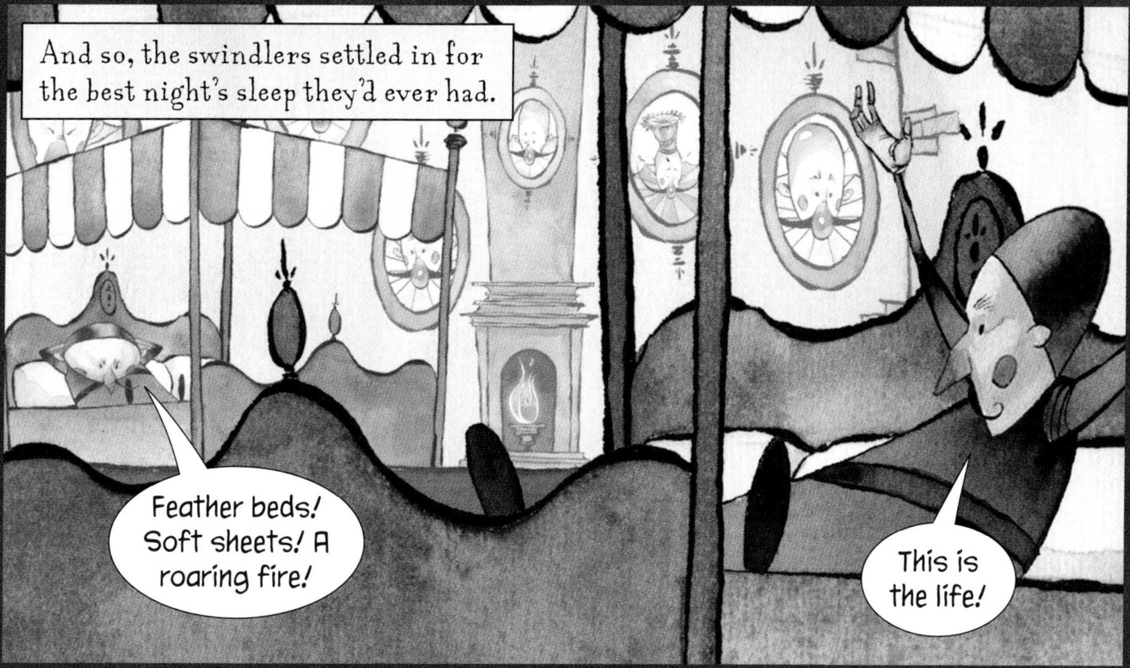
And so, the swindlers settled in for the best night's sleep they'd ever had.
Feather beds! Soft sheets! A roaring fire!
This is the life!

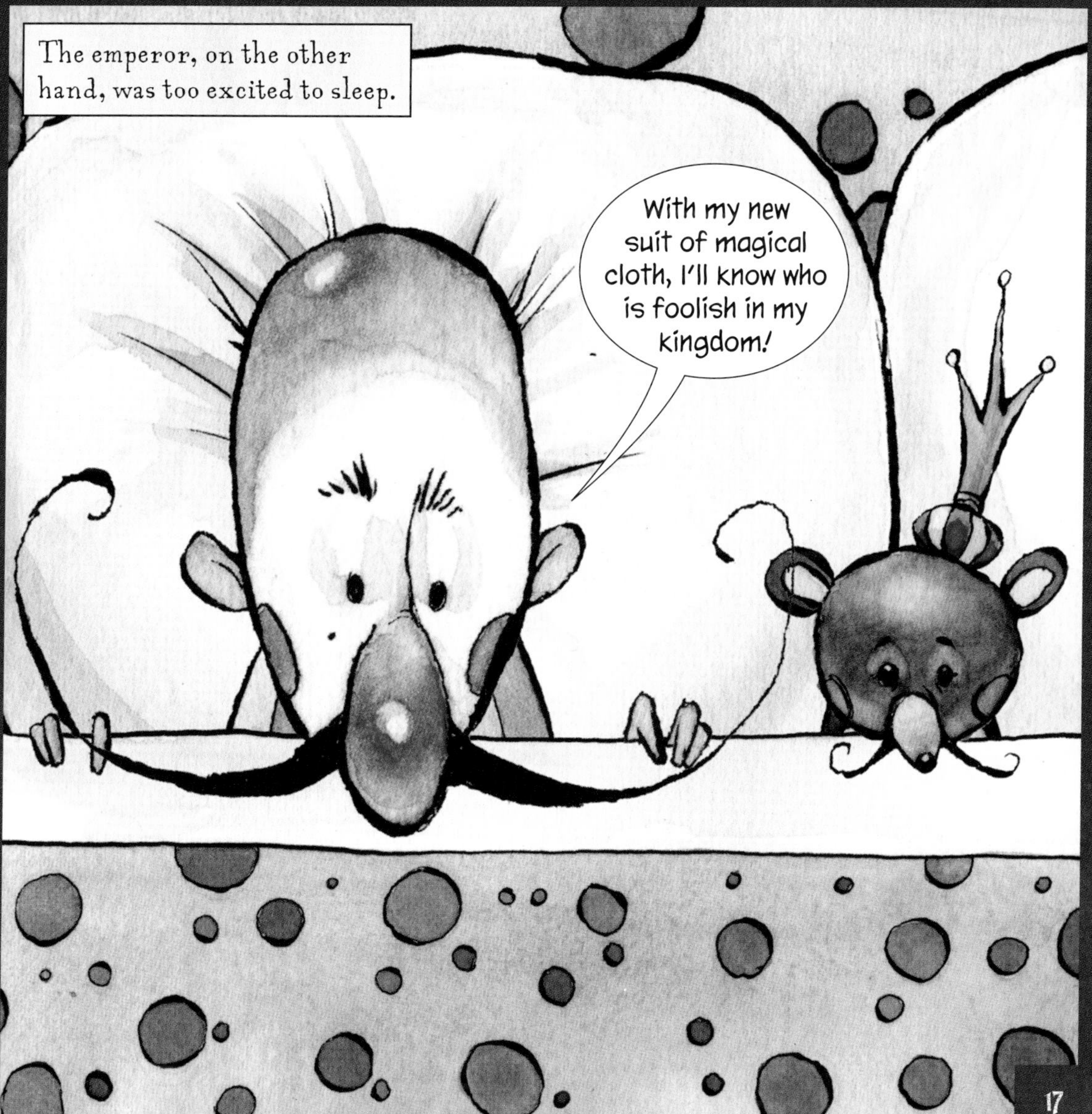
The emperor, on the other hand, was too excited to sleep.
With my new suit of magical cloth, I'll know who is foolish in my kingdom!

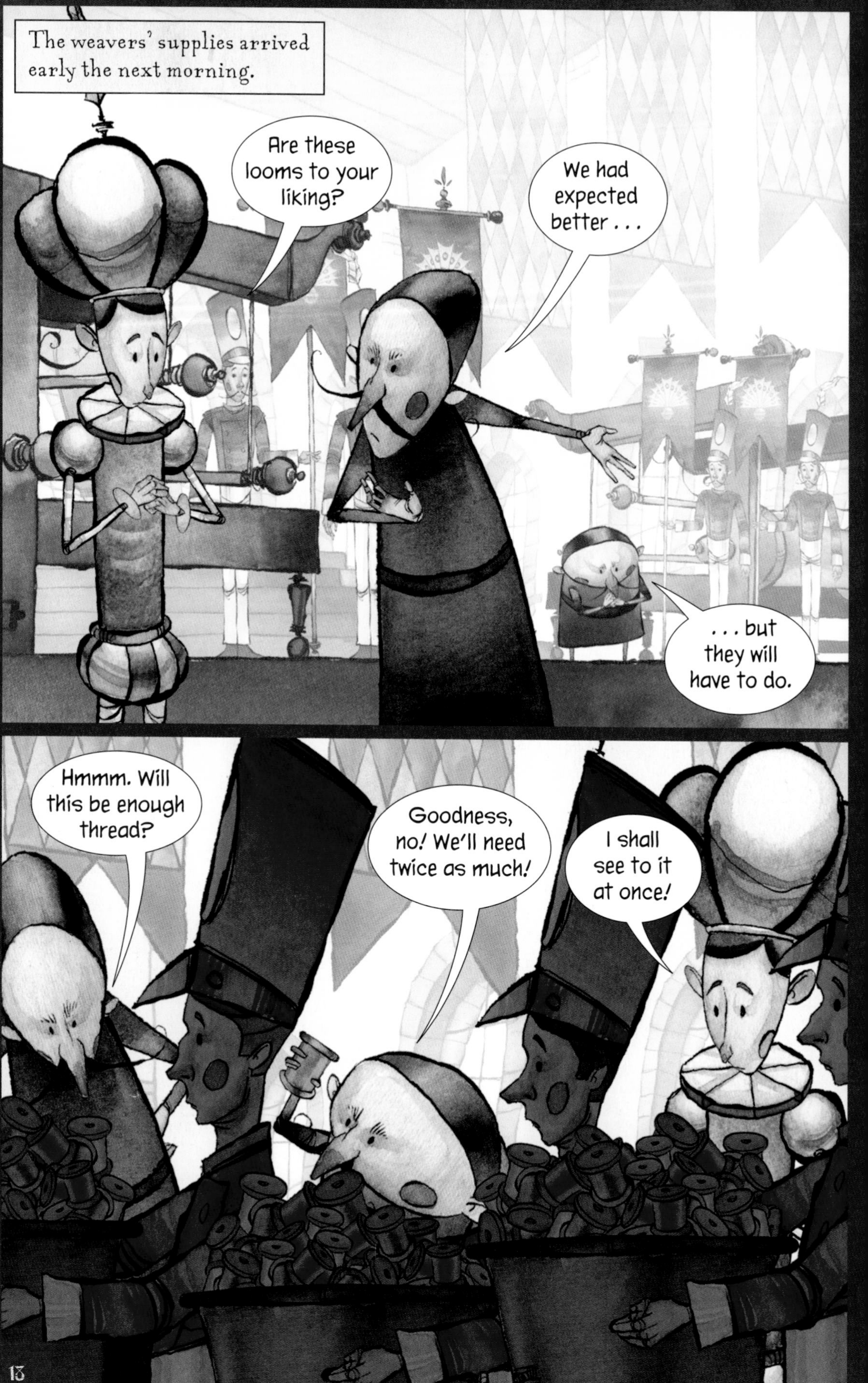
The weavers' supplies arrived early the next morning.
Are these looms to your liking?
We had expected better . . .
. . . but they will have to do.
Hmmm. Will this be enough thread?
Goodness, no! We'll need twice as much!
I shall see to it at once!

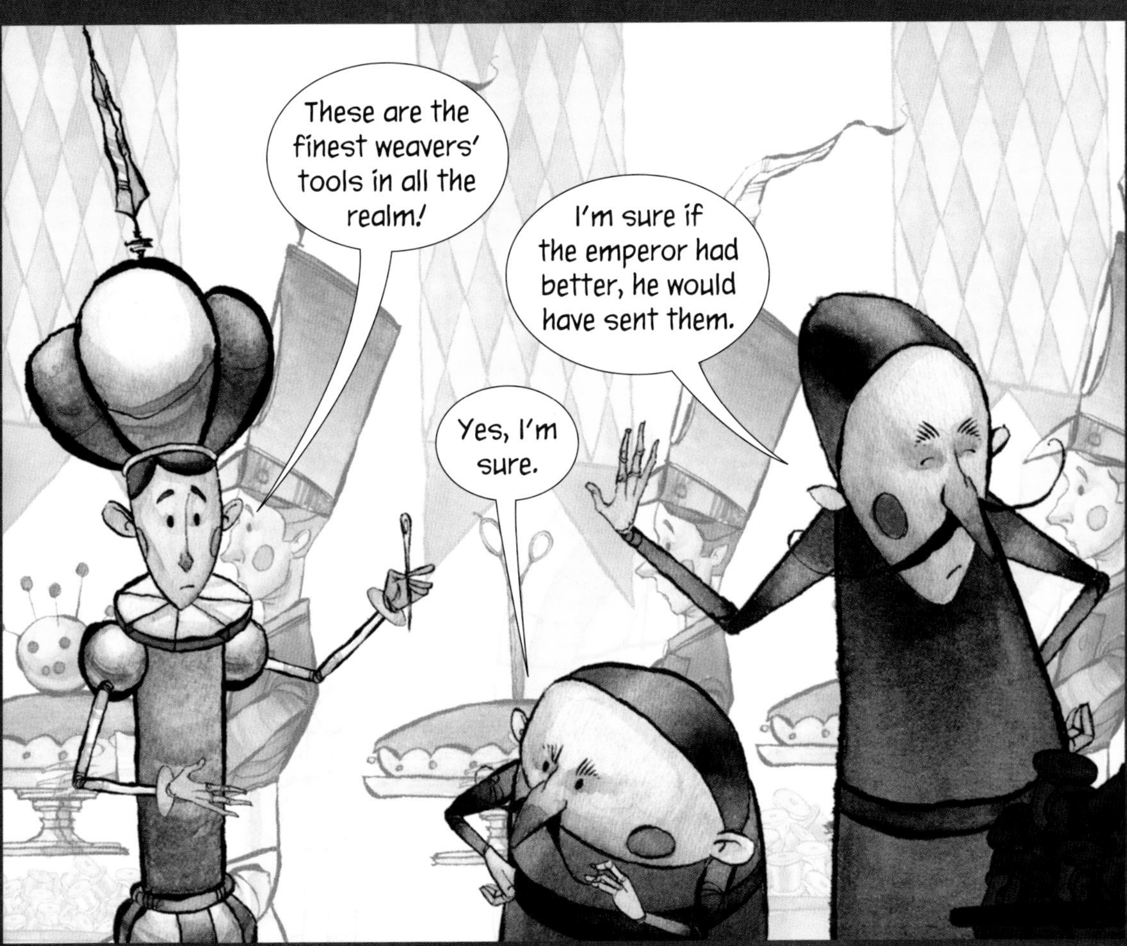
These are the finest weavers' tools in all the realm!
Yes, I'm sure.
I'm sure if the emperor had better, he would have sent them.

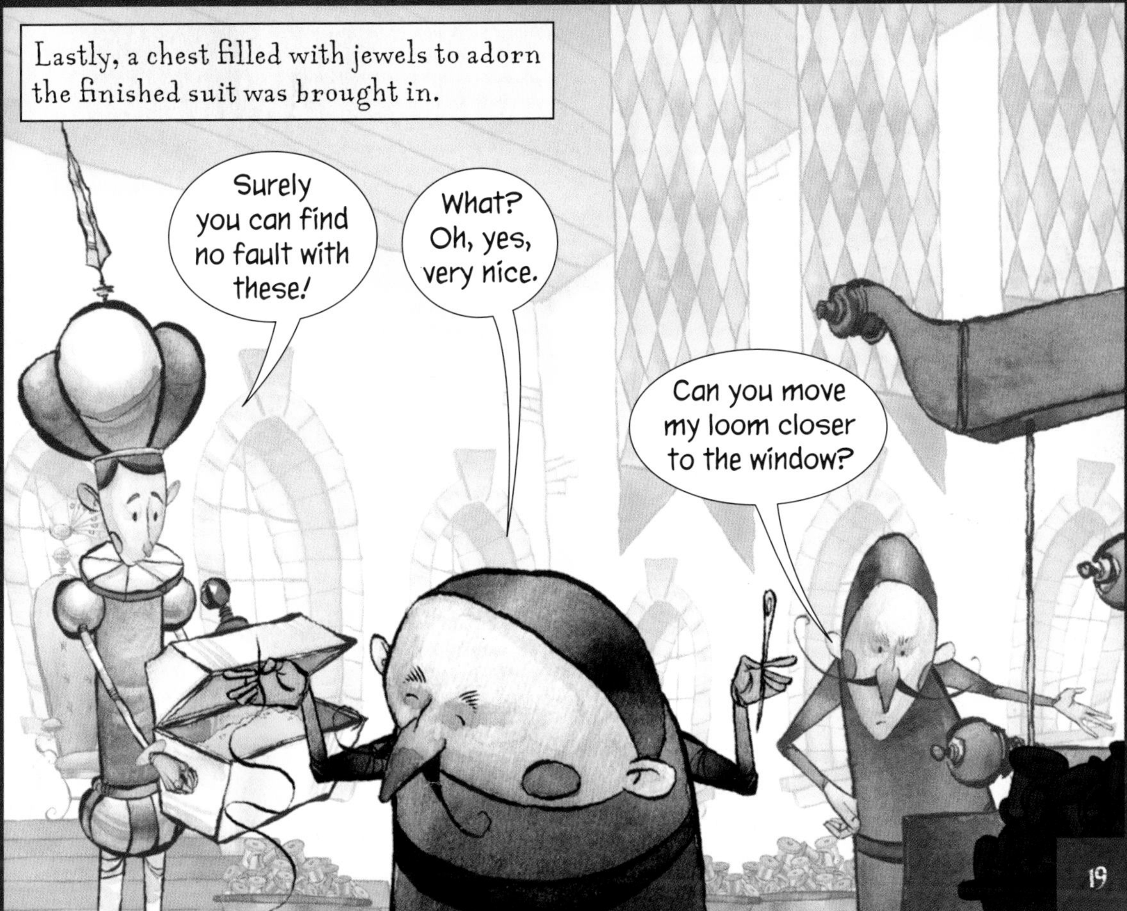
Lastly, a chest filled with jewels to adorn the finished suit was brought in.
Surely you can find no fault with these!
What? Oh, yes, very nice.
Can you move my loom closer to the window?

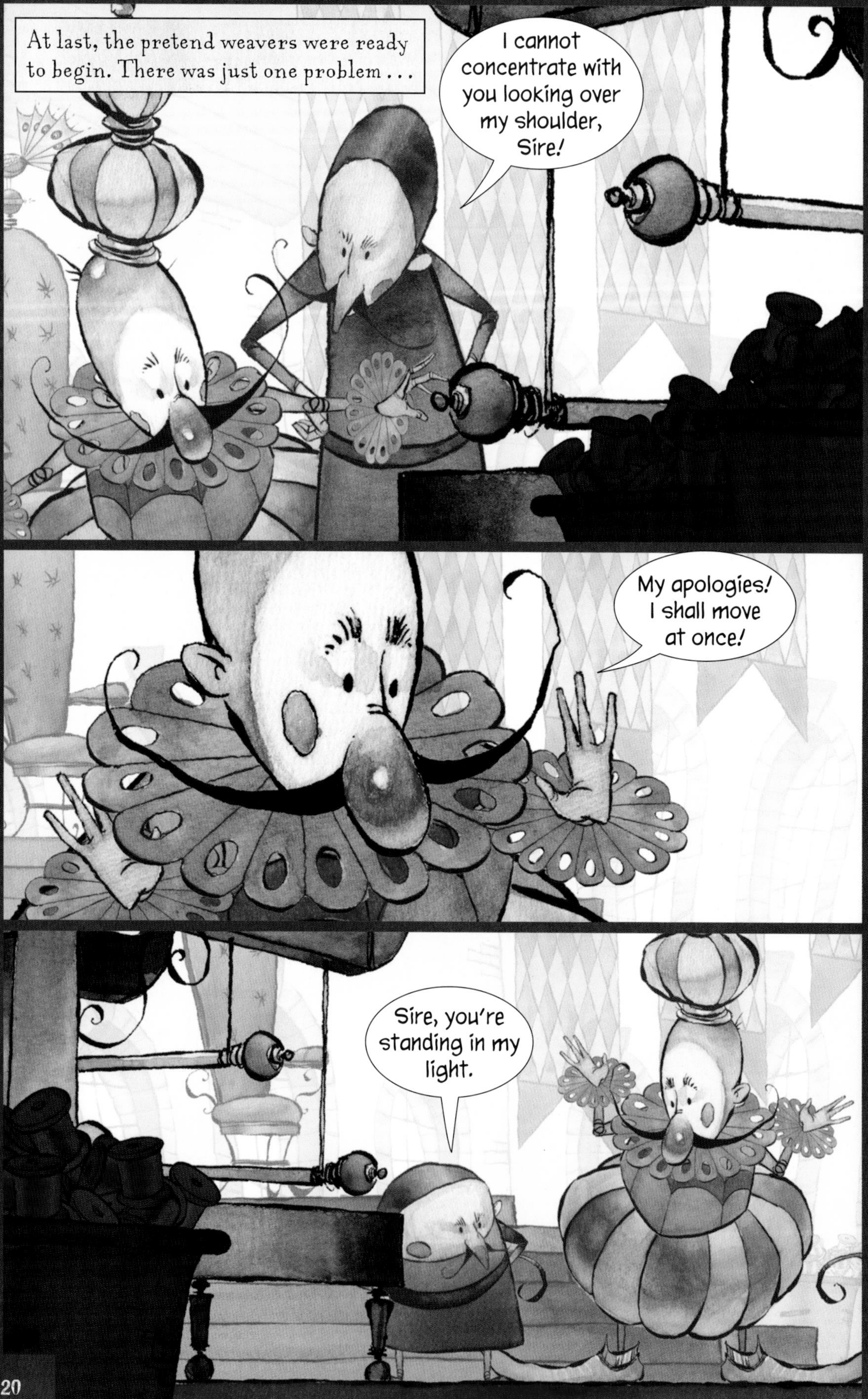
At last, the pretend weavers were ready to begin. There was just one problem . . .
I cannot concentrate with you looking over my shoulder, Sire!
My apologies! I shall move at once!
Sire, you're standing in my light.

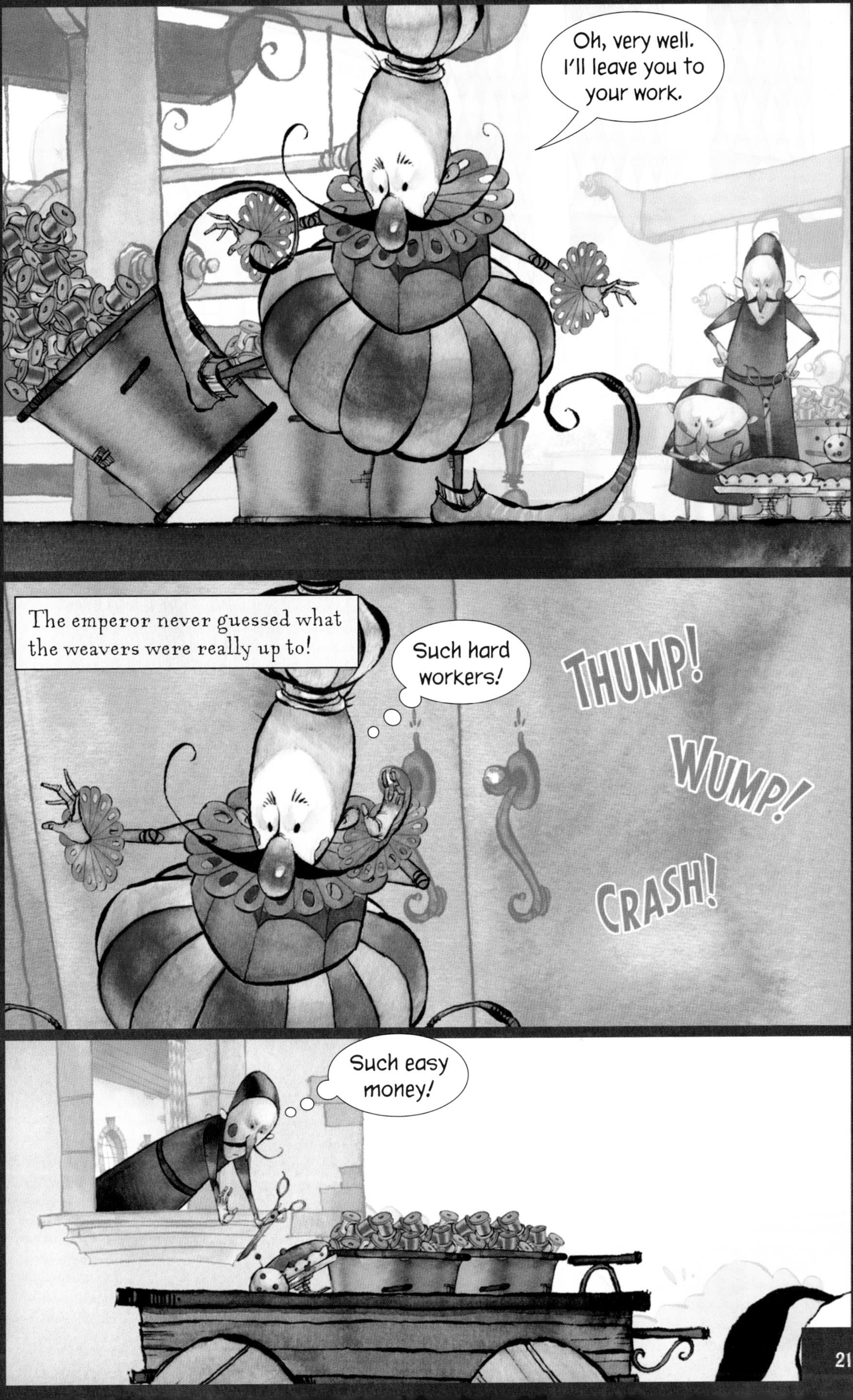
Oh, very well. I'll leave you to your work.
The emperor never guessed what the weavers were really up to!
Such hard workers!
THUMP!
WUMP!
CRASH!
Such easy money!

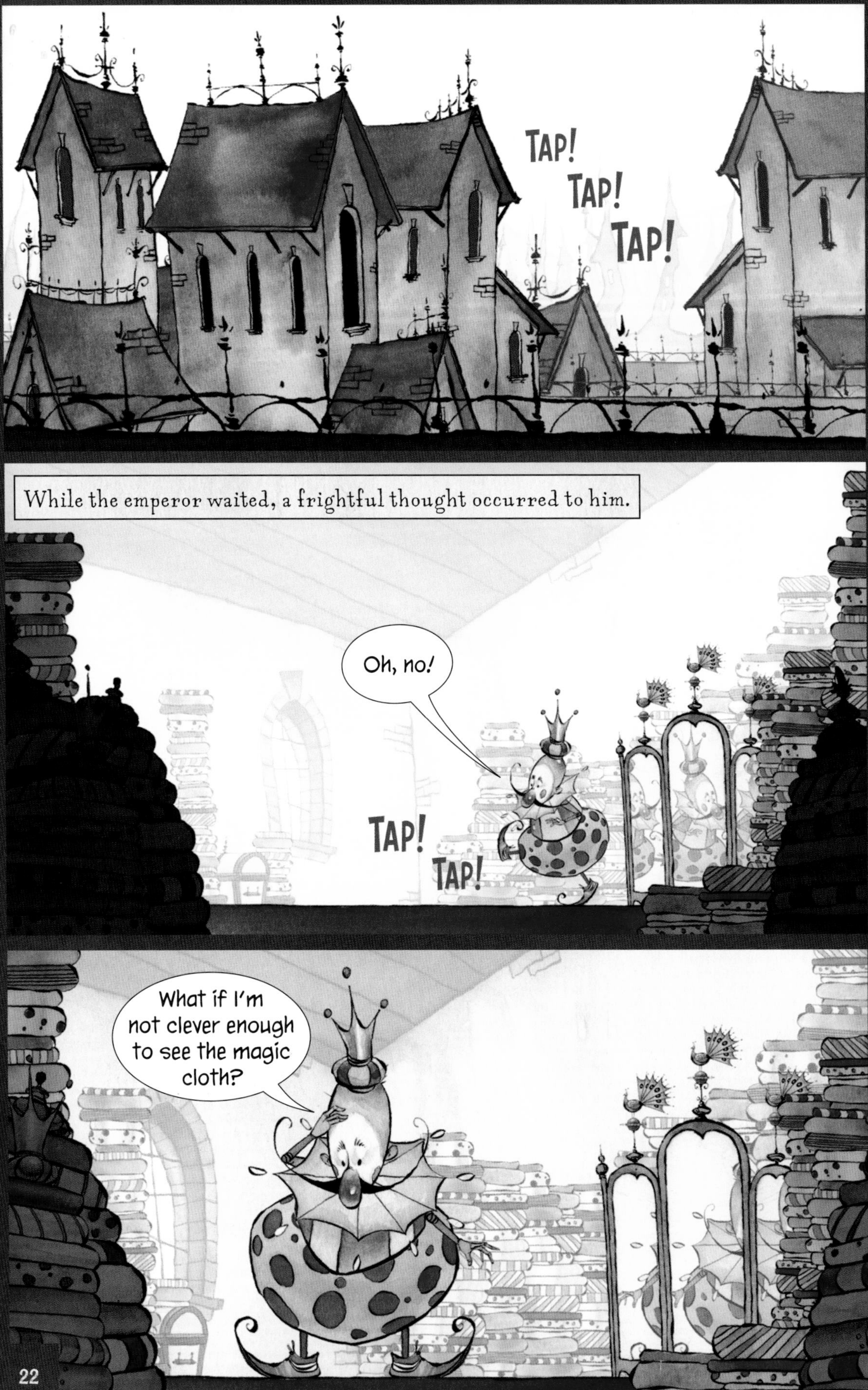
TAP!
TAP!
TAP!
While the emperor waited, a frightful thought occurred to him.
Oh, no!
TAP!
TAP!
What if I'm not clever enough to see the magic cloth?

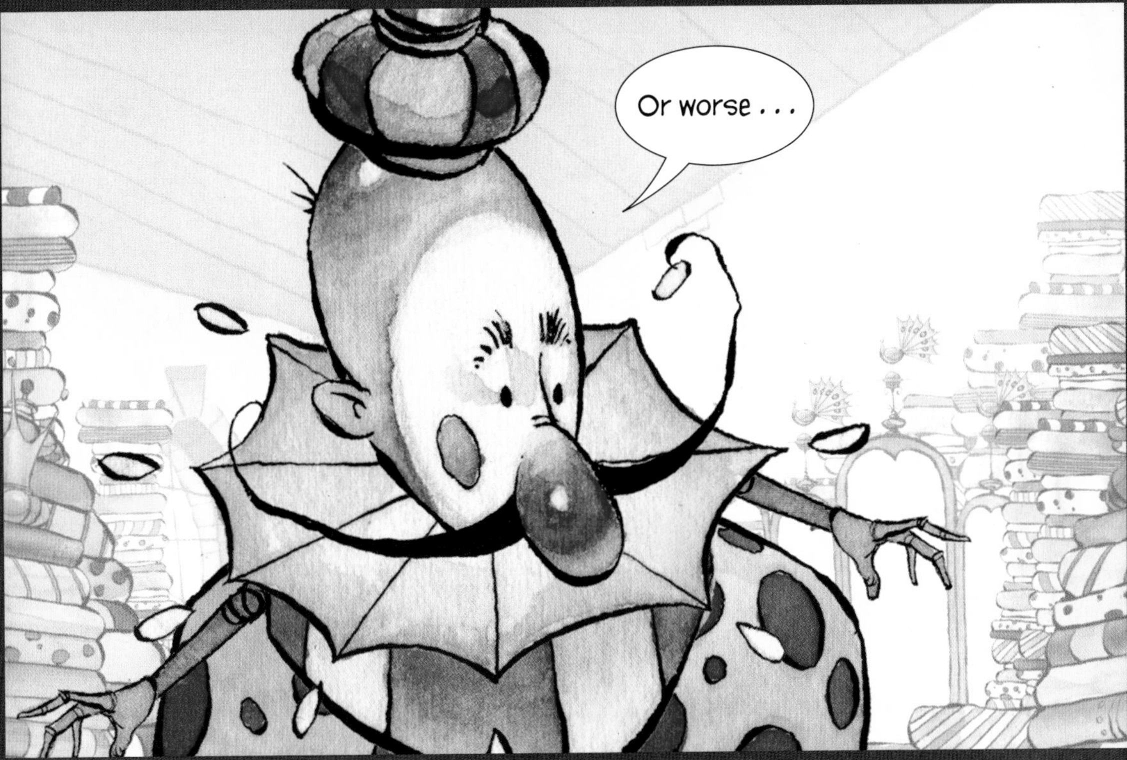
Or worse . . .

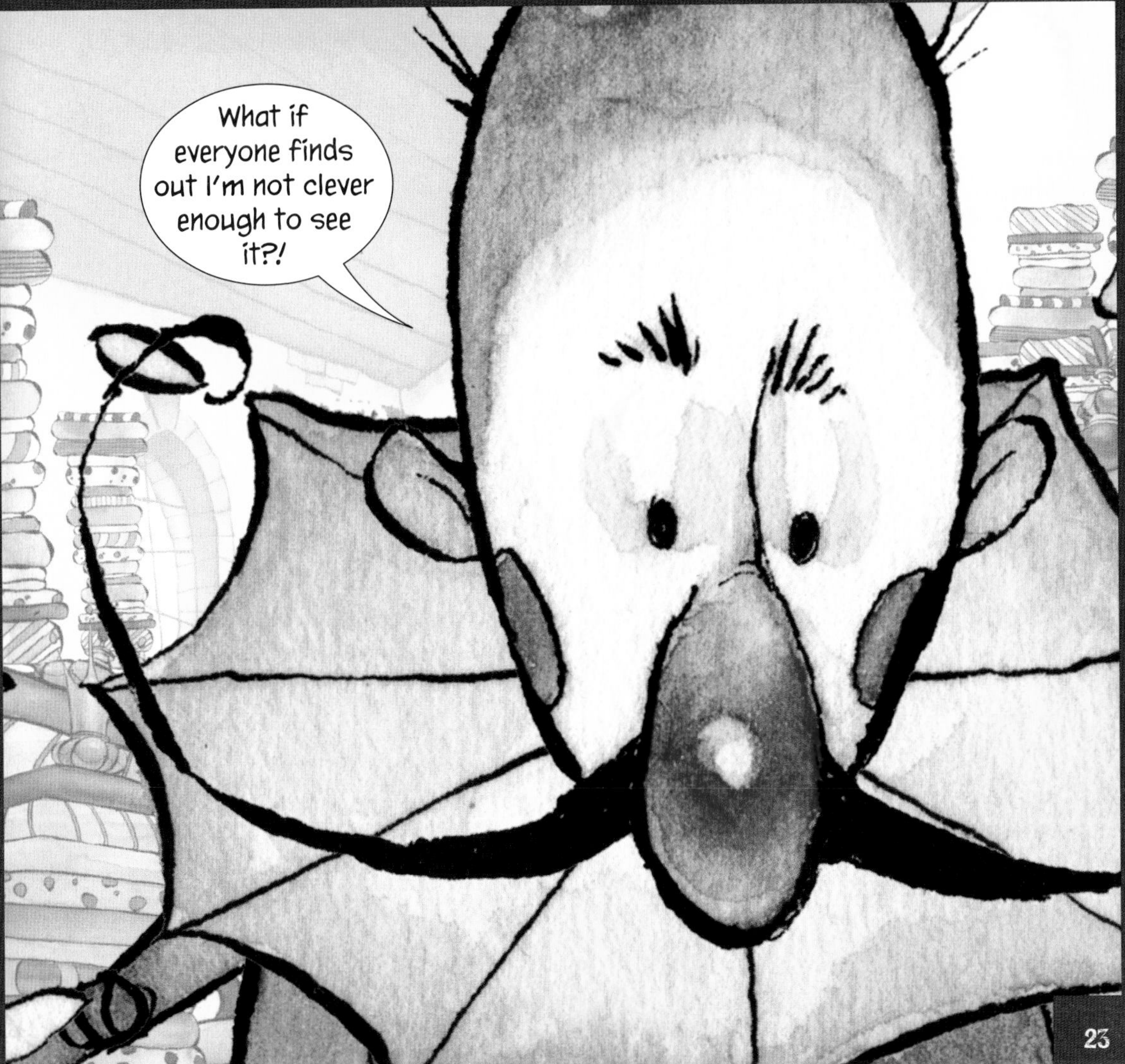
What if everyone finds out I'm not clever enough to see it?!

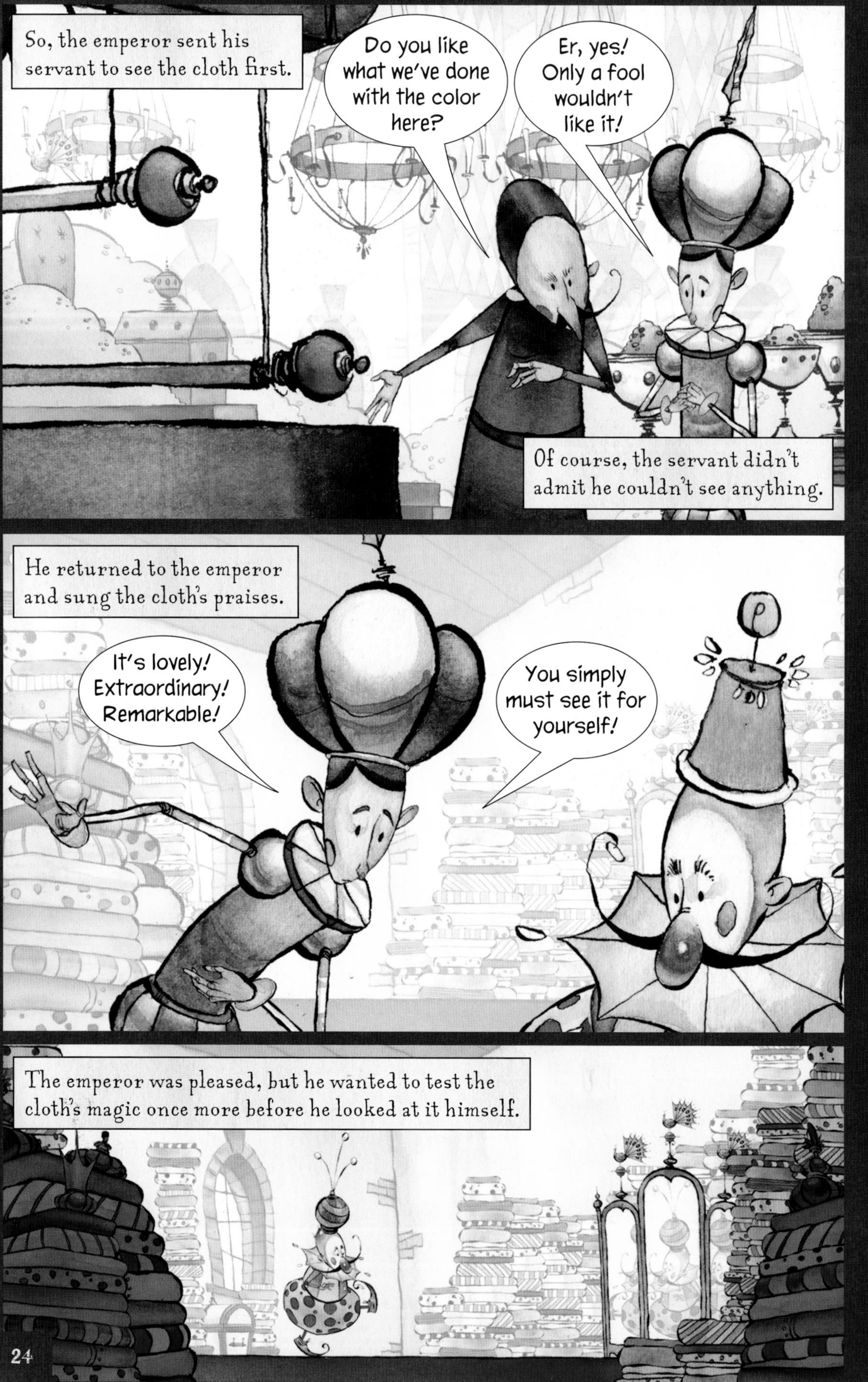
So, the emperor sent his servant to see the cloth first.
Do you like what we've done with the color here?
Er, yes! Only a fool wouldn't like it!
Of course, the servant didn't admit he couldn't see anything.
He returned to the emperor and sung the cloth's praises.
It's lovely! Extraordinary! Remarkable!
You simply must see it for yourself!
The emperor was pleased, but he wanted to test the cloth's magic once more before he looked at it himself.

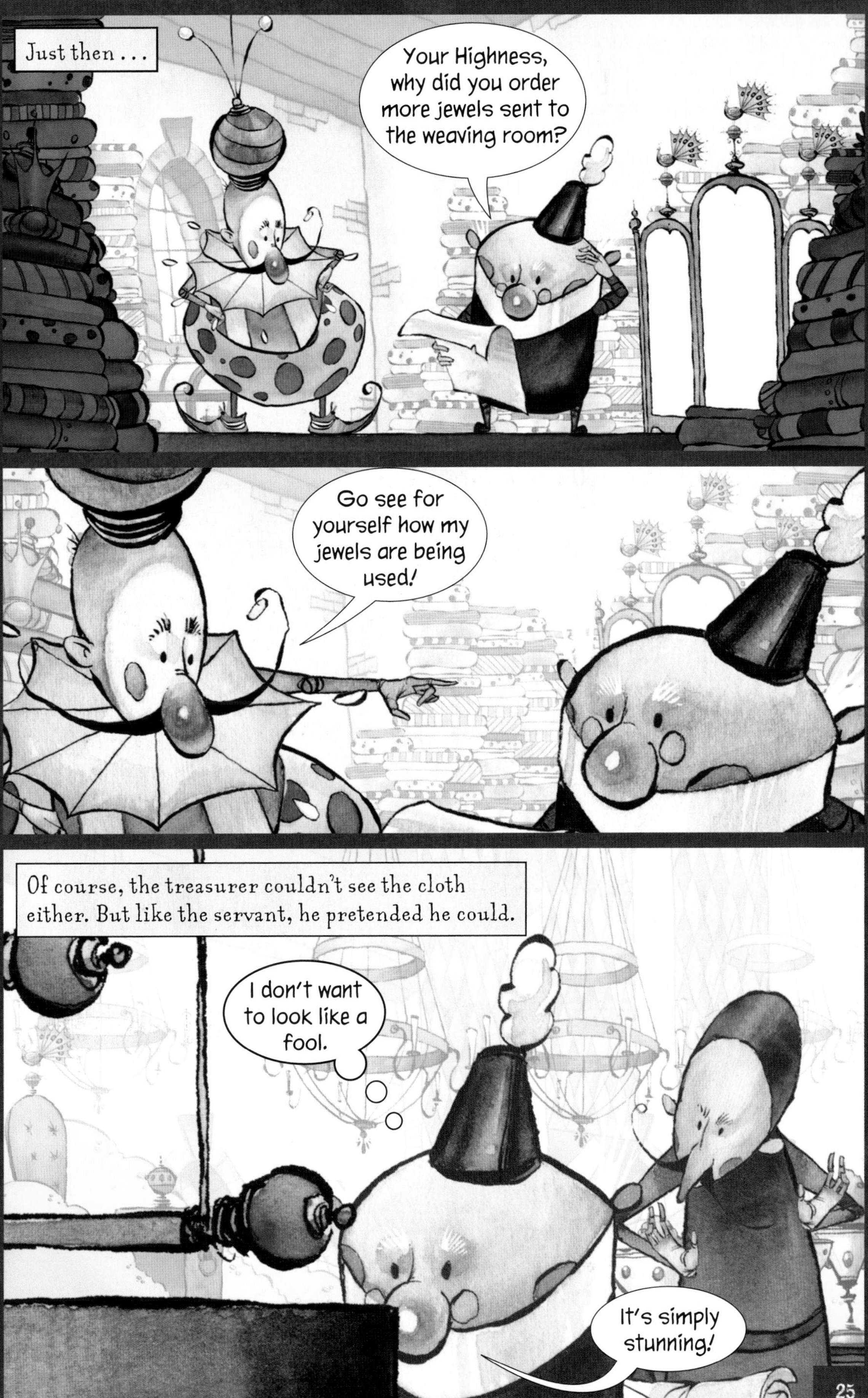
Just then . . .
Your Highness, why did you order more jewels sent to the weaving room?
Go see for yourself how my jewels are being used!
Of course, the treasurer couldn't see the cloth either. But like the servant, he pretended he could.
I don't want to look like a fool.
It's simply stunning!

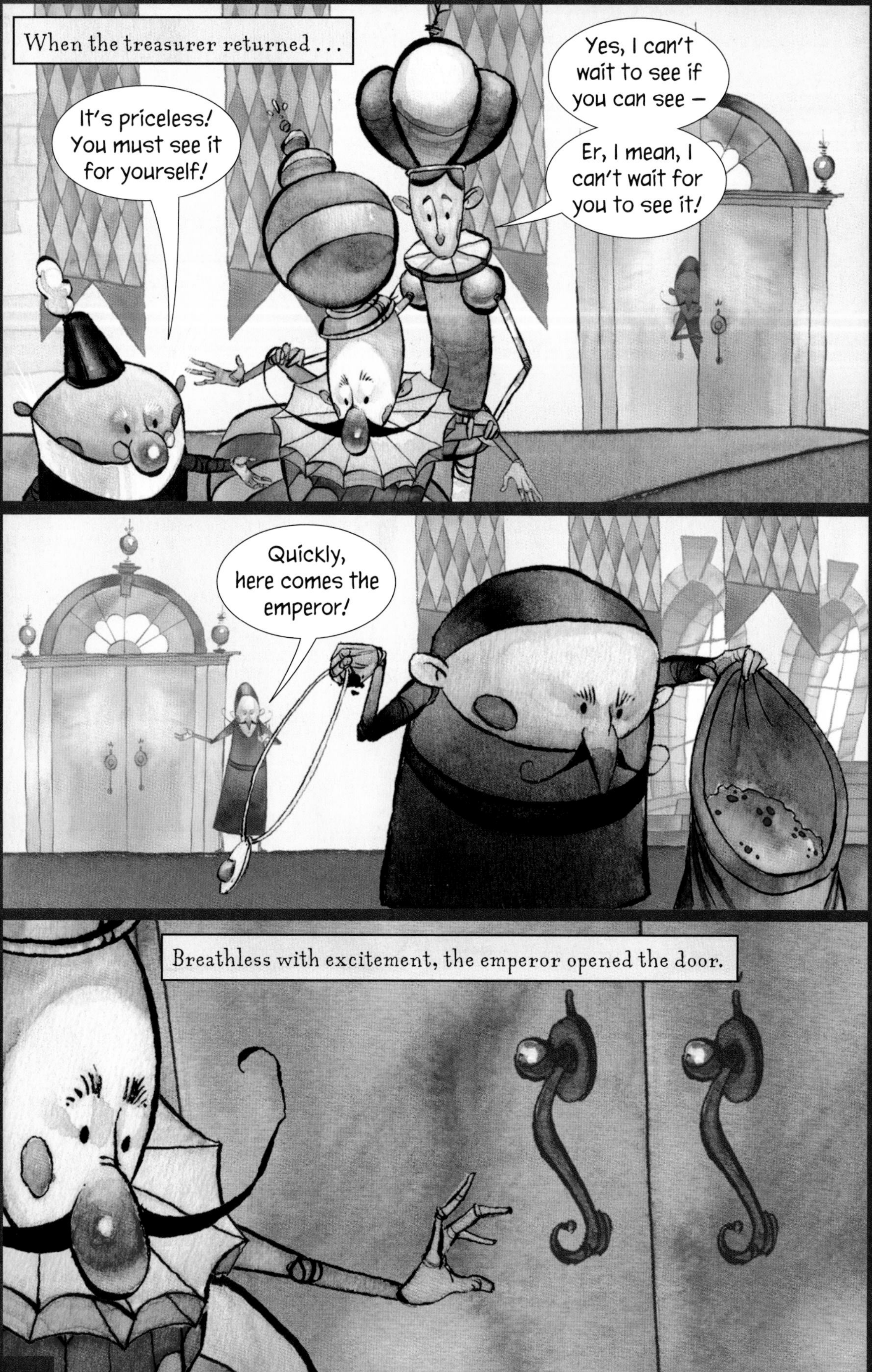
When the treasurer returned . . .
It's priceless! You must see it for yourself!
Yes, I can't wait to see if you can see —
Er, I mean, I can't wait for you to see it!
Quickly, here comes the emperor!
Breathless with excitement, the emperor opened the door.

He peered inside to see . . .

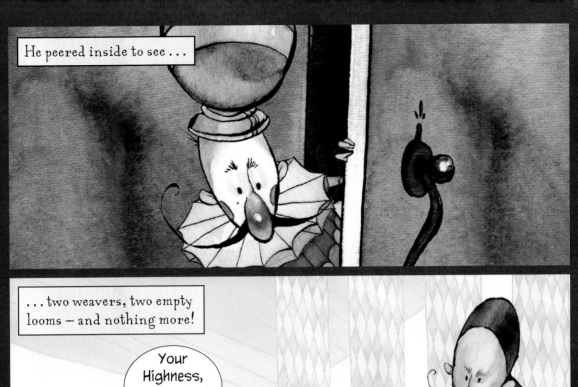

. . . two weavers, two empty looms — and nothing more!

Your Highness, you are just in time!

As you can *clearly* see, we are done weaving!

Of course, the emperor couldn't see the cloth at all. But he knew better than to say so!

See how it shimmers!

So soft! So delicate!

It looks exactly like I imagined it! Begin my suit at once!

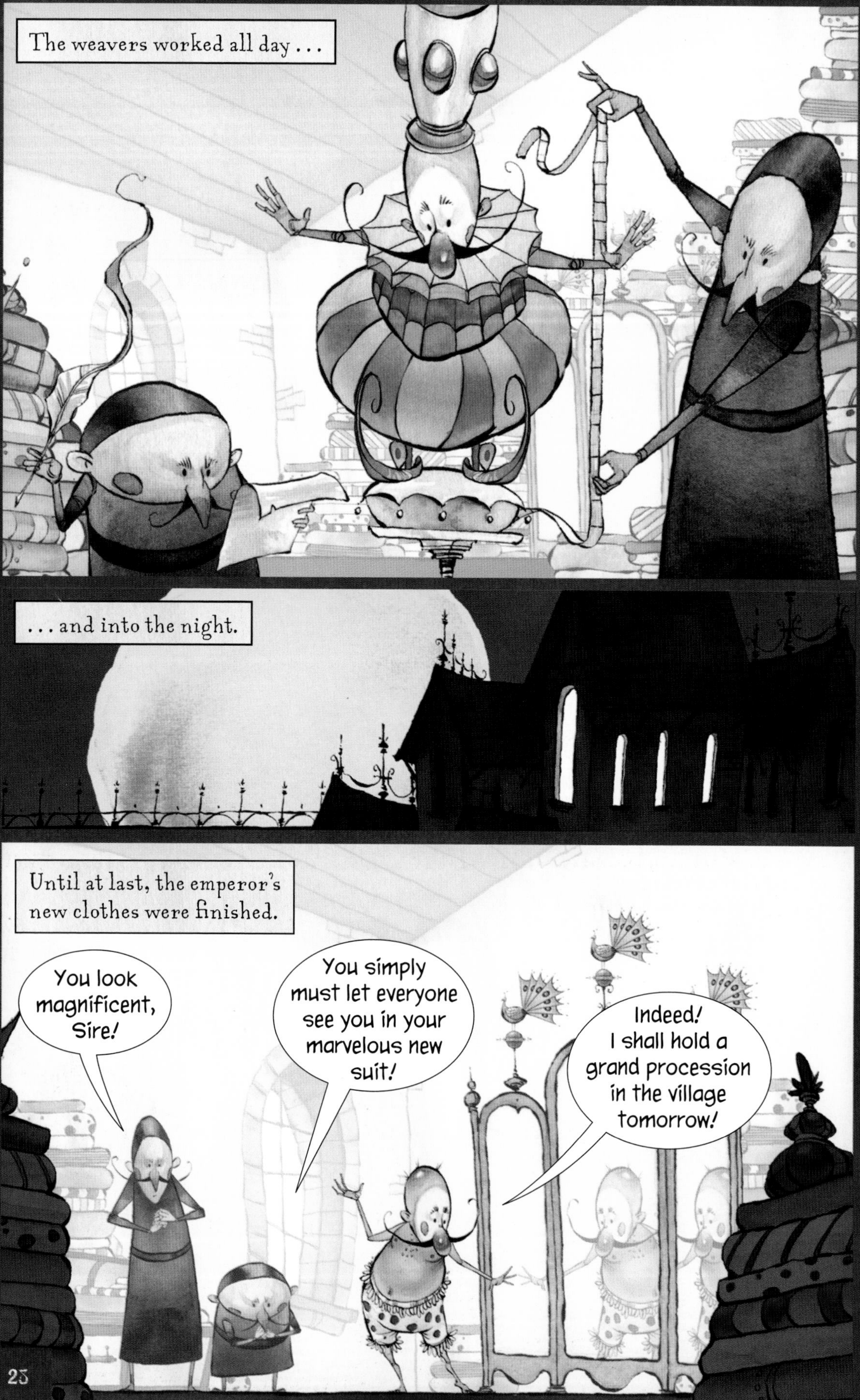
The weavers worked all day . . .
. . . and into the night.
Until at last, the emperor's new clothes were finished.
You look magnificent, Sire!
You simply must let everyone see you in your marvelous new suit!
Indeed! I shall hold a grand procession in the village tomorrow!

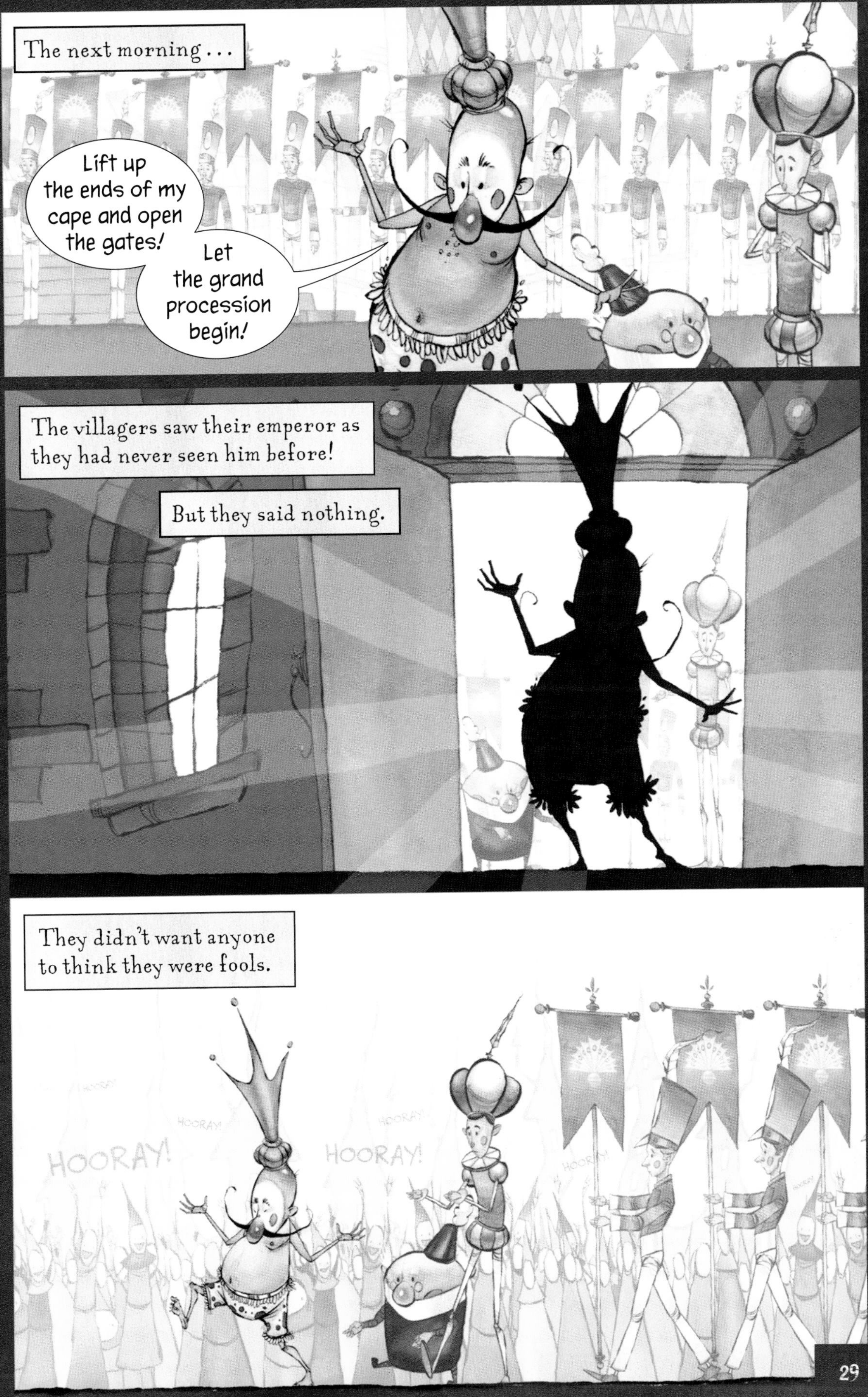
The next morning . . .
Lift up the ends of my cape and open the gates!
Let the grand procession begin!
The villagers saw their emperor as they had never seen him before!
But they said nothing.
They didn't want anyone to think they were fools.
HOORAY!
HOORAY!

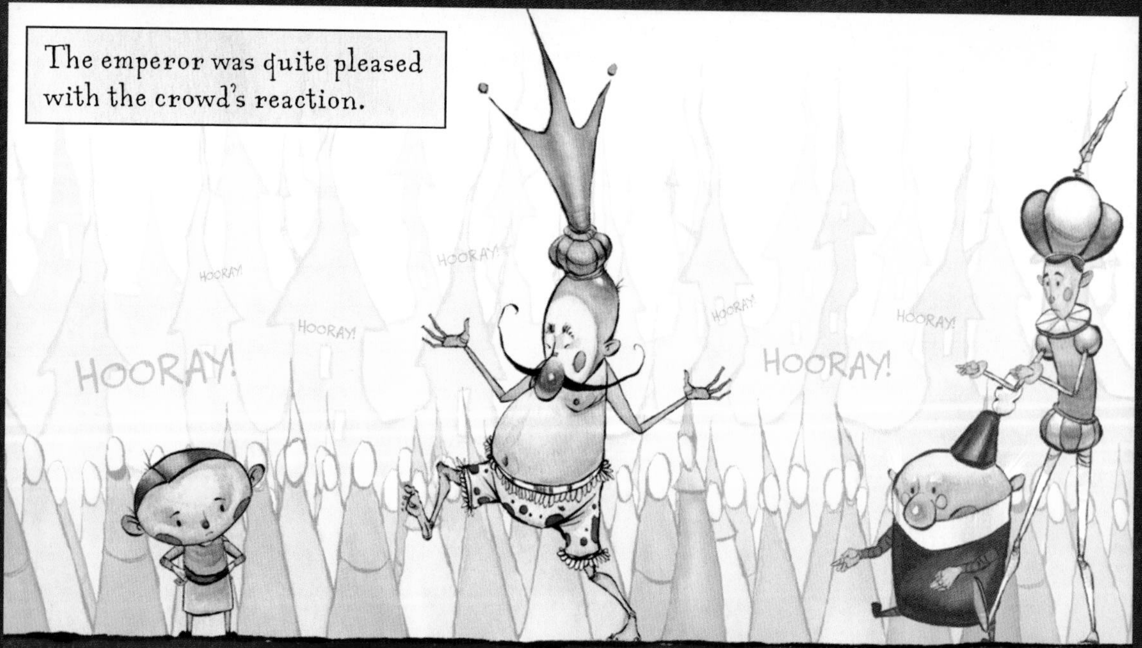
The emperor was quite pleased with the crowd's reaction.
HOORAY!
HOORAY!
HOORAY!
HOORAY!
HOORAY!
HOORAY!
HOORAY!

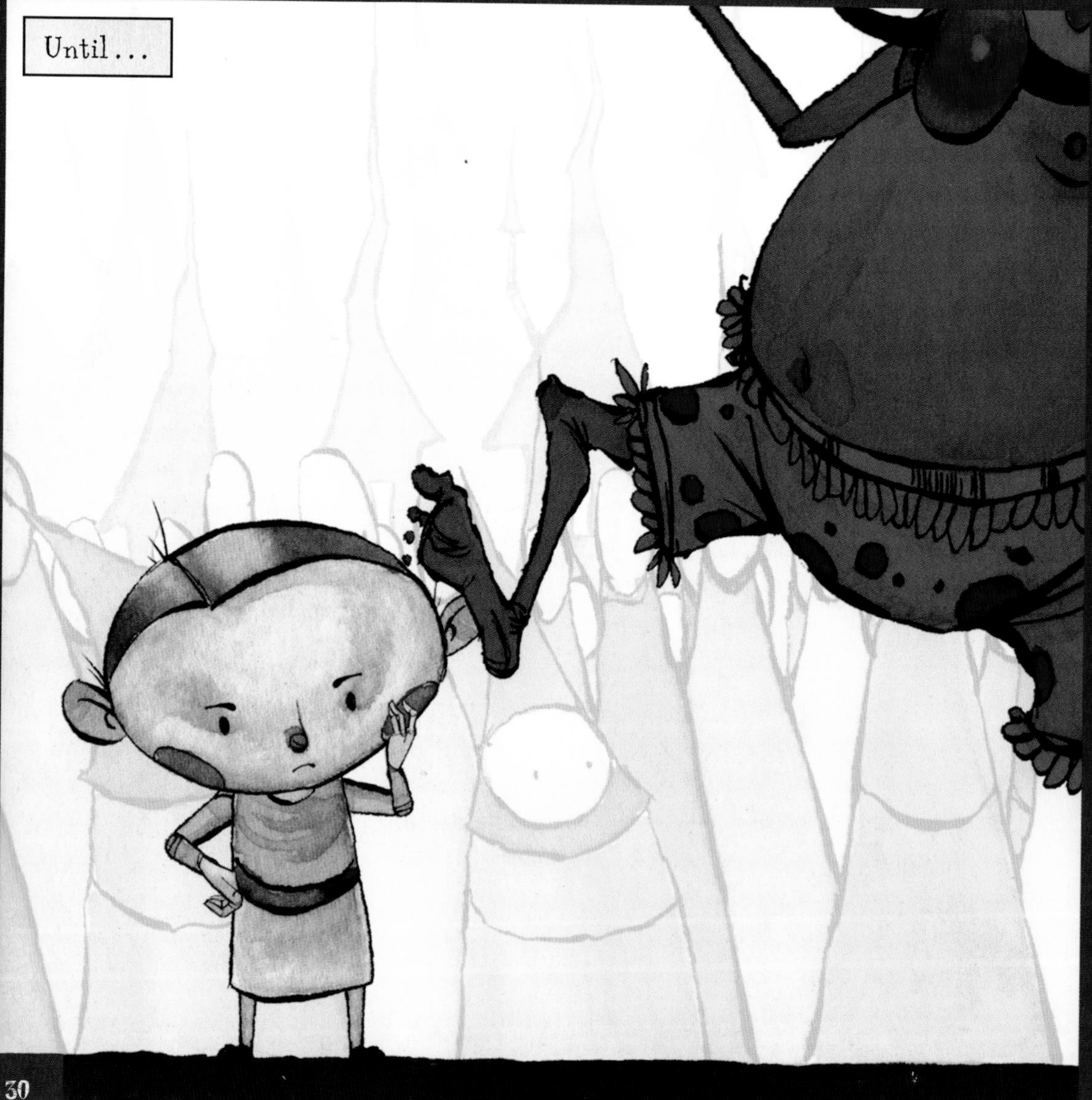
Until . . .

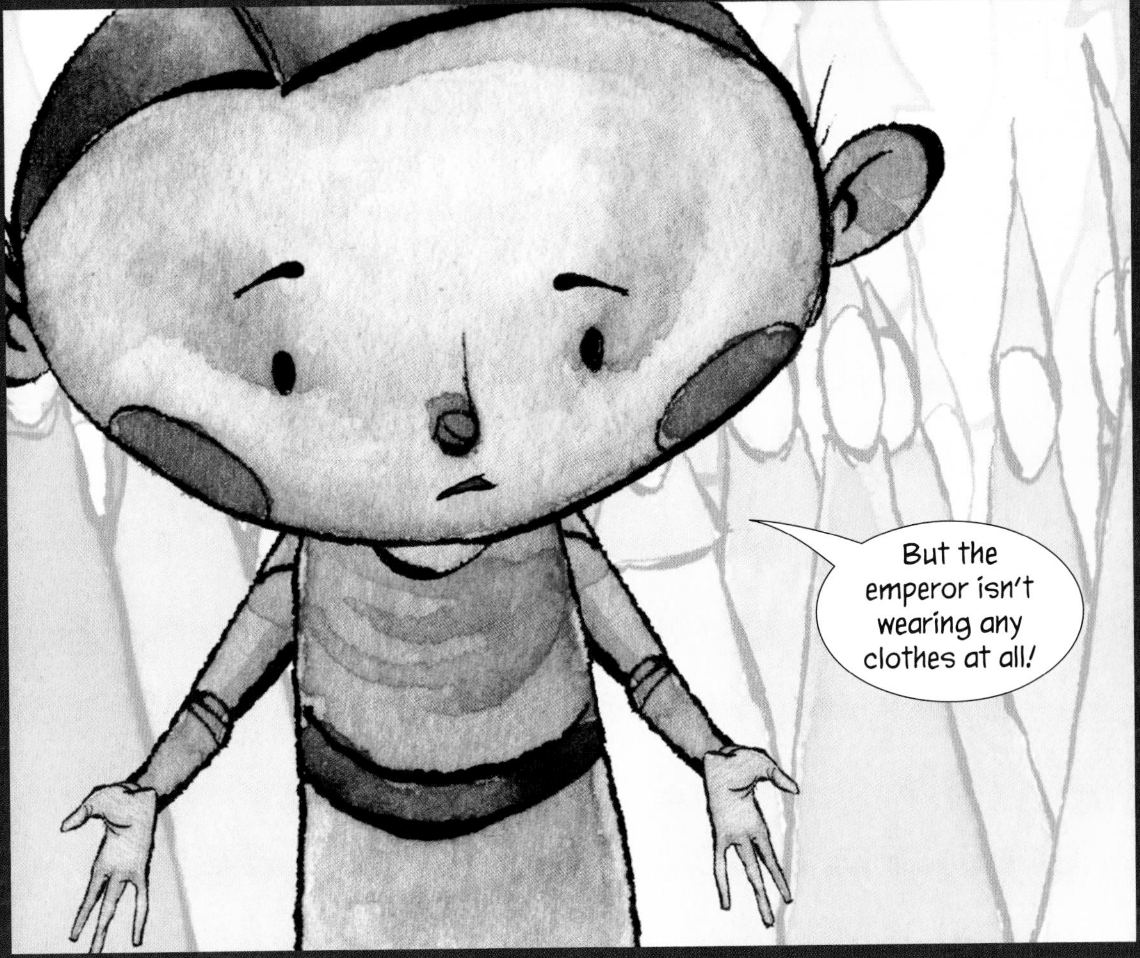
But the emperor isn't wearing any clothes at all!
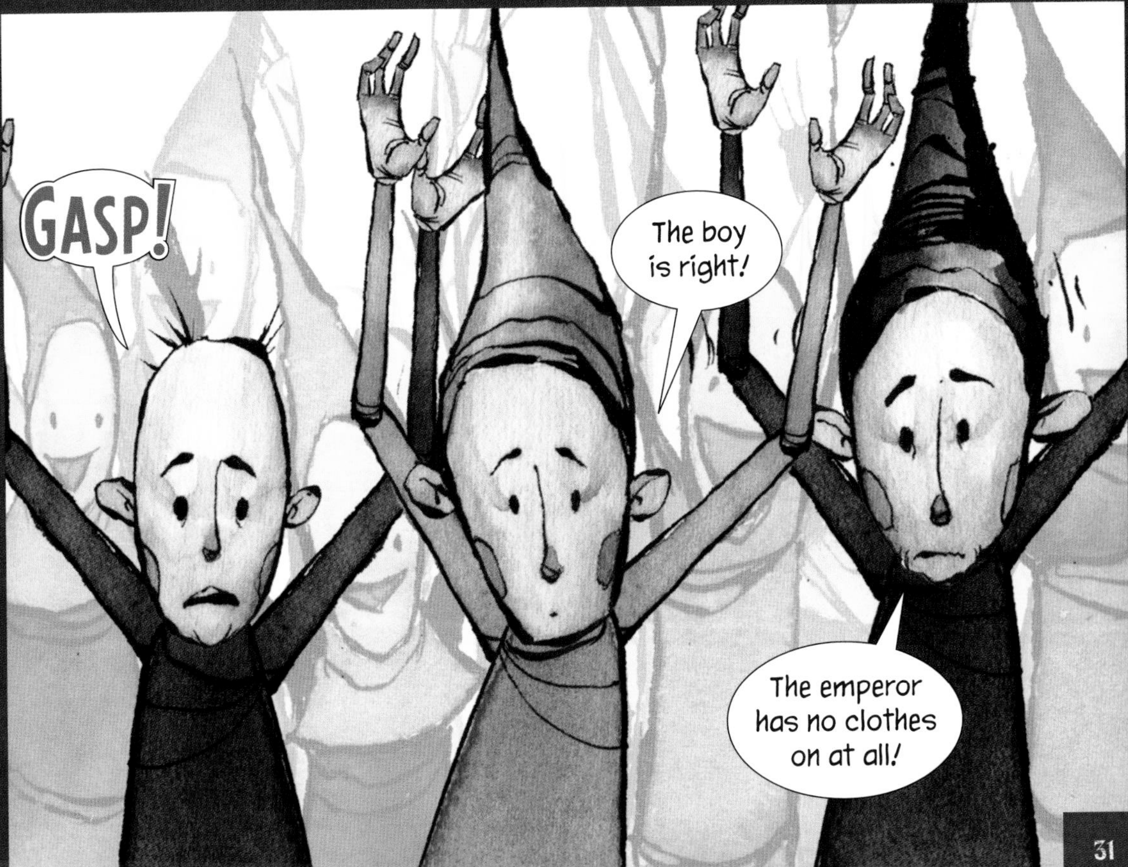
GASP!
The boy is right!
The emperor has no clothes on at all!

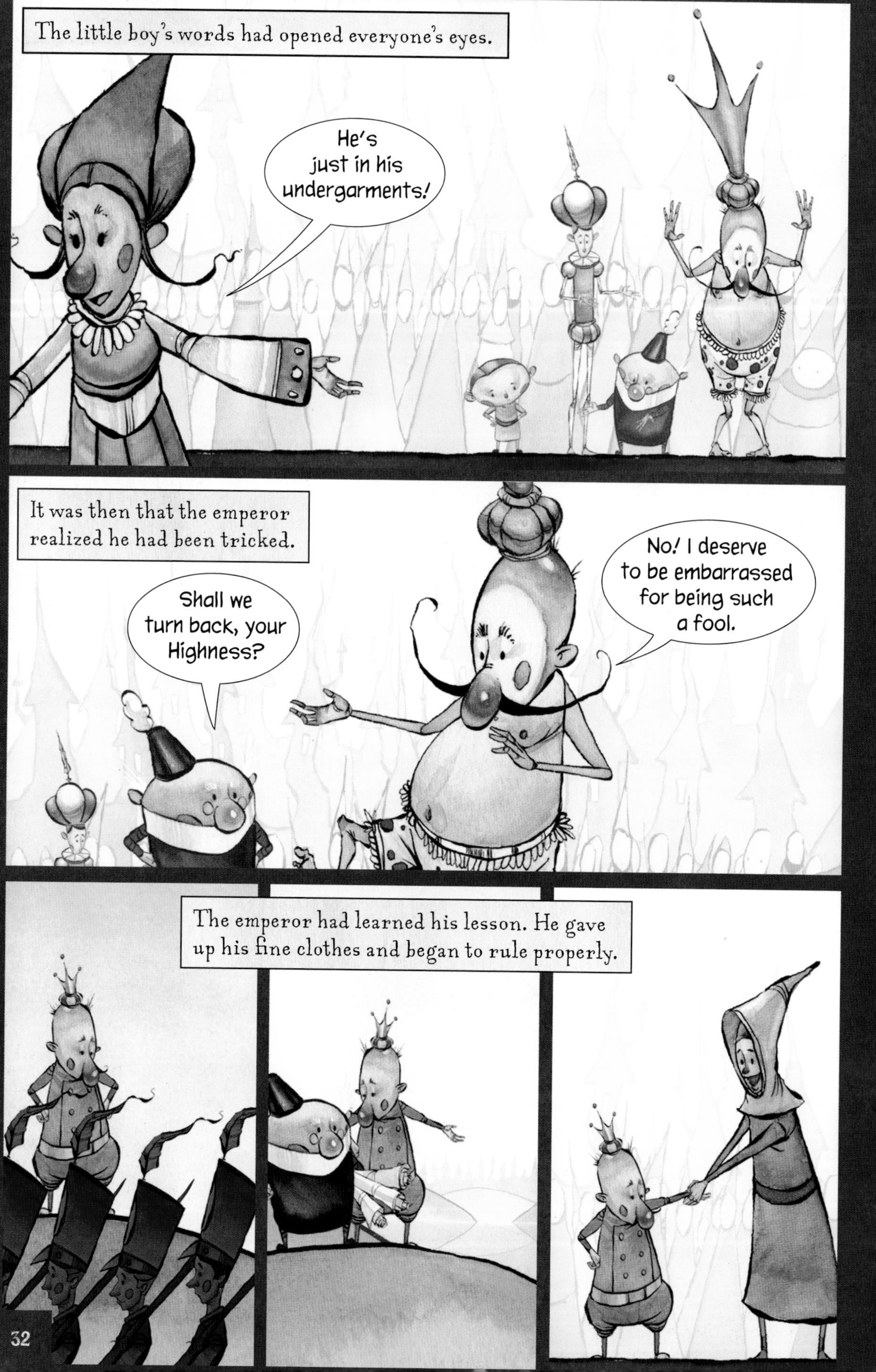
The little boy's words had opened everyone's eyes.
He's just in his undergarments!
It was then that the emperor realized he had been tricked.
Shall we turn back, your Highness?
No! I deserve to be embarrassed for being such a fool.
The emperor had learned his lesson. He gave up his fine clothes and began to rule properly.

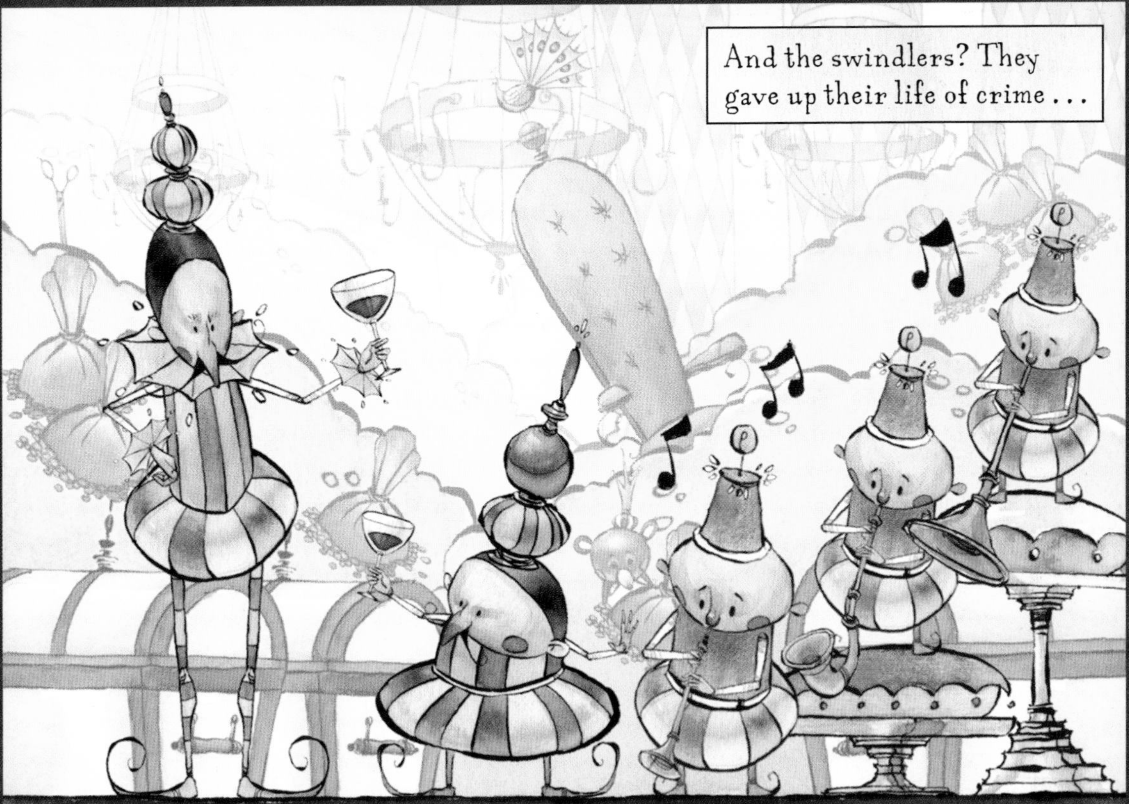
And the swindlers? They gave up their life of crime . . .

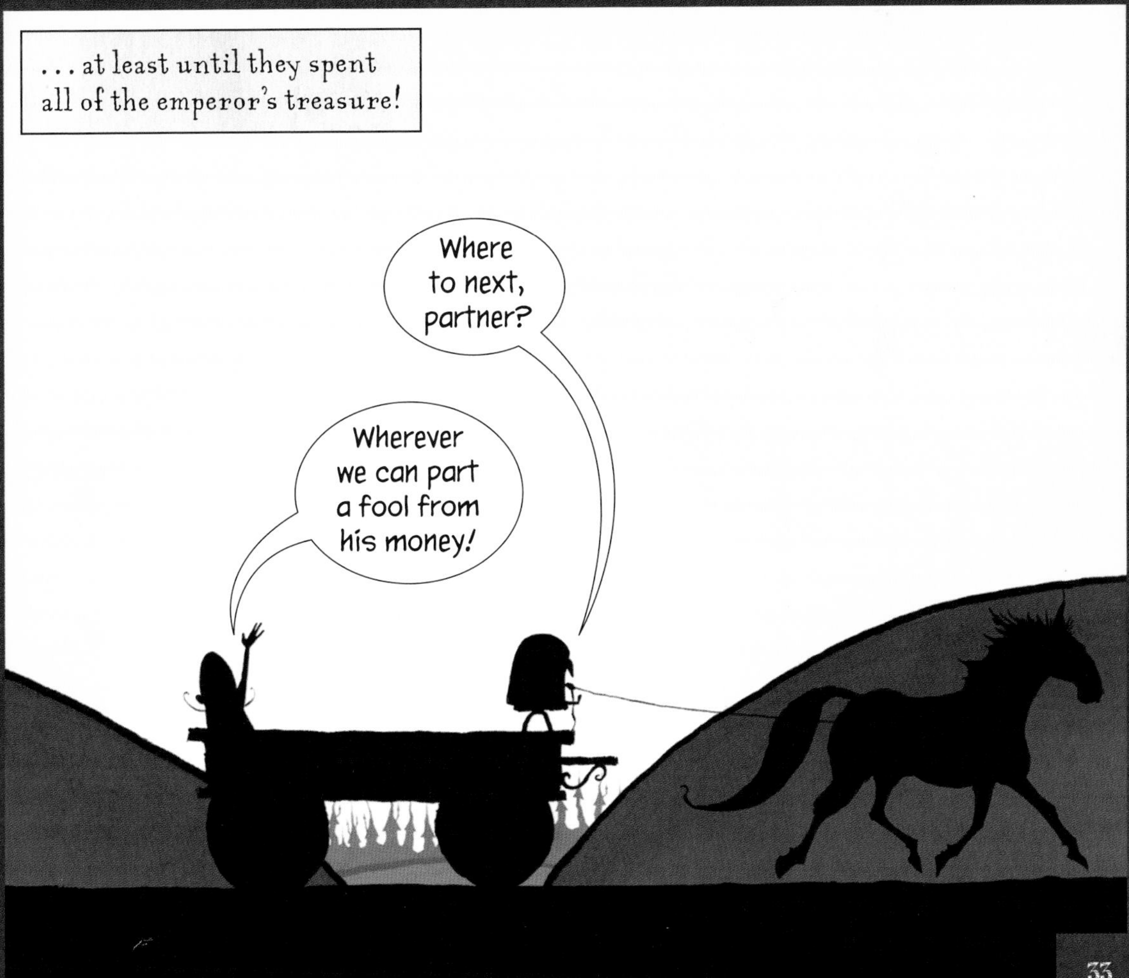
. . . at least until they spent all of the emperor's treasure!
Where to next, partner?
Wherever we can part a fool from his money!

glossary

ADORN (uh-DORN)—to decorate or add beauty to something

ATTIRE (uh-TIRE)—clothing

DELICATE (DEL-uh-kuht)—finely made and fragile

GARMENTS (GAR-muhntz)—pieces of clothing

INSISTED (in-SIST-id)—demanded something

INSPECTED (in-SPEKT-id)—looked at something very carefully

PROCESSION (pruh-SESH-uhn)—a number of people walking along as part of a parade

SHIMMERS (SHIM-urz)—shines with a faint, steady light

SIRE (SYE-ur)—a respectful term of address for a male ruler

SUBJECTS (SUHB-jiktz)—people who live in a kingdom under the rule of a king or queen

WARDROBE (WORD-robe)—a collection of clothes belonging to one person

about the author

Hans Christian Andersen was born in Odense, Denmark, on April 2, 1805. As Hans grew up, he tried many different professions, but none seemed to fit. He eventually found work as an actor and singer, but when his voice changed, he could no longer sing well enough to make a living. Then, a friend suggested that he start writing. A short time later, he published his first story, "The Ghost at Palnatoke's Grave."

Andersen's first book of fairy tales was published in 1835. He continued to write children's stories, publishing one almost every year, until he fell ill in 1872. Andersen had written more than 150 fairy tales before his death in 1875. He is considered to be the father of the modern fairy tale.

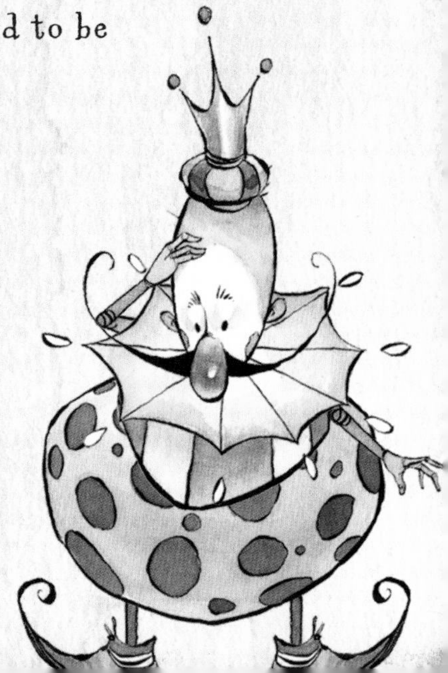

about the retelling author

After working more than 10 years as a children's book editor, Stephanie True Peters started writing books herself. She has since written 40 books, including the New York Times best seller *A Princess Primer: A Fairy Godmother's Guide to Being a Princess*. When not at her computer, Peters enjoys playing with her two children, hitting the gym, or working on home improvement projects with her patient and supportive husband, Daniel.

about the illustrator

Jeffrey Stewart Timmins was born July 2, 1979. In 2003, he graduated from the Classical Animation program at Sheridan College in Oakville, Ontario. He currently works as a freelance designer and animator. Even as an adult, Timmins still holds onto a few important items from his childhood, such as his rubber boots, cape, and lenseless sunglasses.

discussion questions

1. Why do you think it took so long for someone to point out that the emperor wasn't wearing any clothes?

2. Emperors are chosen by birth. Presidents are chosen by elections. Which way of choosing a leader do you think is better? Why?

3. If the Swindlers were caught, what do you think would be a fair punishment for them? Jail? A fine? Something else?

writing prompts

1. Imagine that you're an emperor. What kinds of laws would you make? Would you be a strict and stern ruler, or a kind and caring ruler? Write about your kingdom.

2. The Swindlers make money by tricking other people. Have you ever been tricked? What did you do about it? How did it make you feel?

3. At the end of the book, the Swindlers ran out of money. Do you think it was wise to spend it so quickly? What would you have done with all that wealth?

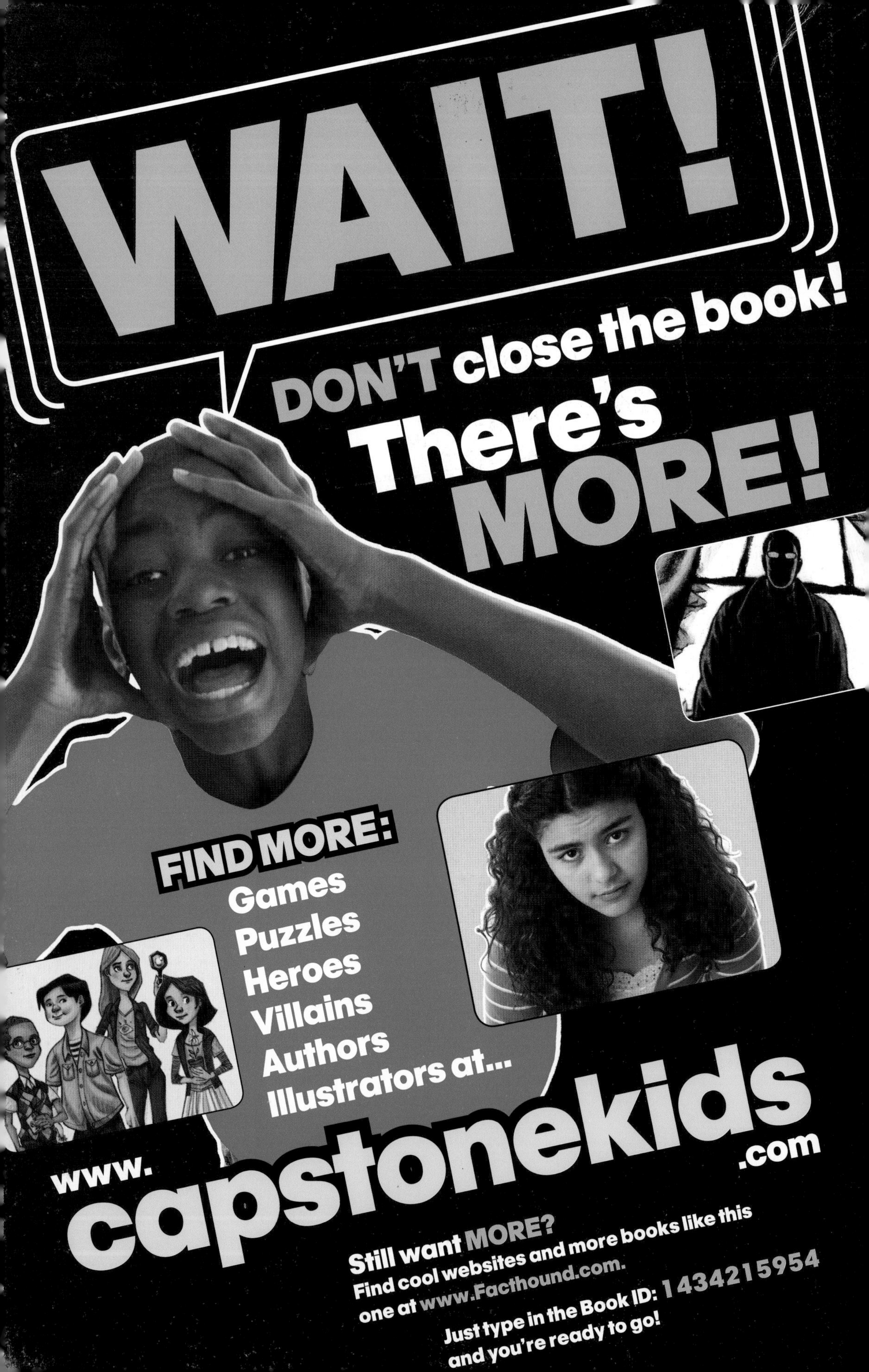
WAIT!
DON'T close the book!
There's MORE!
FIND MORE:
Games
Puzzles
Heroes
Villains
Authors
Illustrators at...
www.
capstonekids
.com
Still want MORE?
Find cool websites and more books like this one at www.Facthound.com.
Just type in the Book ID: 1434215954
and you're ready to go!